The Mahabharata

Also by R. K. Narayan

NOVELS OF MALGUDI

Swami and Friends
The Bachelor of Arts
The Dark Room
The English Teacher
Mr Sampath—The Printer of Malgudi
The Financial Expert
Waiting for the Mahatma
The Guide
The Man-Eater of Malgudi
The Vendor of Sweets
The Painter of Signs
A Tiger for Malgudi
Malgudi Days
Talkative Man

The Ramayana
The Mahabharata
The World of Nagaraj

STORIES

A Horse and Two Goats
An Astrologer's Day and Other Stories
Lawley Road
Under the Banyan Tree and Other Stories
The Grandmother's Tale and Selected Stories

MEMOIRS

My Days

TRAVEL

My Dateless Diary
The Emerald Route

ESSAYS

Next Sunday
Reluctant Guru

The Mahabharata

A Shortened Modern Prose Version of the Indian Epic

R. K. Narayan

Foreword by Wendy Doniger

WITH DECORATIONS BY R. K. LAXMAN

THE UNIVERSITY OF CHICAGO PRESS * *Chicago & London*

R. K. NARAYAN (1906–2001) was one of the most prominent Indian novelists of the twentieth century. His works include *Mr. Sampath—The Printer of Malgudi, Swami and Friends, Waiting for Mahatma,* and *Gods, Demons, and Others,* all published by the University of Chicago Press.

WENDY DONIGER is an American Indologist and the Mircea Eliade Distinguished Service Professor of the History of Religions in the Divinity School of the University of Chicago. She is the author of more than thirty books.

The University of Chicago Press, Chicago 60637
The University of Chicago Press, Ltd., London
 Originally published 1978 by the Viking Press.
University of Chicago Press edition 2000 and 2013
Printed in the United States of America

22 21 20 19 18 17 3 4 5

ISBN-13: 978-0-226-05165-9 (paper)
ISBN-13: 978-0-226-05747-7 (e-book)
DOI: 10.7208/chicago/9780226057477.001.001

Library of Congress Cataloging-in-Publication Data

Narayan, R. K., 1906–2001.
The Mahabharata : a shortened modern prose version of the Indian epic / R. K. Narayan ; foreword by Wendy Doniger.
pages. cm.
ISBN 978-0-226-05165-9 (pbk. : alk. paper) — ISBN 978-0-226-05747-7 (e-book)
1. Hindu mythology—Fiction. 2. Hindu gods—Fiction. 3. Mahabharata—Adaptations.
I. Doniger, Wendy. II. Title.
PR9499.3.N3M3 2013
823'.912—dc23

2013005614

This paper meets the requirements of ANSI/NISO Z39.48-1992 (Permanence of Paper).

CONTENTS

FOREWORD

Poets have told it before, and are telling it now, and will tell it. . . . What is here, about piety, profit, and pleasure, is found elsewhere, but what is *not* here is nowhere else.

Mahabharata (1.1.23 and 1.56.33)

THUS THE *MAHABHARATA* DESCRIBES itself as unlimited in both time and space. Its enormous scope poses two big problems that anyone who tries to translate the *Mahabharata* must confront: choosing the parts to translate, and finding the words to convey the unique spirit of the text. R. K. Narayan succeeds in solving both of these better than any of the dozens of writers who have dared to take on the task.

As for the choice, the *Mahabharata* is not only dauntingly large, as Narayan points out in his own excellent introduction to the first edition of this volume; it also refuses to stand still long enough for anyone to take an accurate picture of it. Although the text was preserved both orally and in manuscript, it is so extremely fluid that there is no single *Mahabharata*; there are hundreds of *Mahabharatas*—hundreds of different manuscripts and innumerable oral versions. A. K. Ramanujan once remarked that no Indian ever hears the *Mahabharata* for the first time; others have described it as a work in progress or a living library that does not belong in a book. There is a soi-disant critical edition of the *Mahabharata*, with an apparatus of "interpolations" longer than the text itself, but that edition has not been able to defend its claim to sit alone on the throne of the urtext. (For instance, the story of the poet Vyasa dictating the *Mahabharata* to the god Ganesha, which everyone who knows anything about the *Mahabharata* knows is a part of it, did not pass the manuscript muster of the critical edition; Narayan tells this story in his introduction, but not in the text.)

The *Mahabharata* flits back and forth between Sanskrit manuscripts and village storytellers, each adding new bits to the old story, constantly reinterpreting it. Narayan is therefore just doing, and doing very well, what others have done for centuries—selecting certain parts of the great text to retell in his own words. One of the fault lines along which others have made such a selection is between the basic linear plot (the tale of the five heroes, the Pandava brothers, and the great war that they fight against their cousins) and the nonlinear blocks of mythology and philosophy that constitute a major part of the *Mahabharata*. Earlier European scholars regarded these parts of the text as irrelevant interpolations, presumably made by devout Brahmins who didn't mind spoiling a good secular story with their pedantic and self-serving religious rants. But none of this is true: the plot is not secular, to begin with, as the gods are caught up with it at every moment; nor are the myths and philosophical arguments extraneous to it. Indeed, for a Hindu reader (or listener), the myths and debates (including such things as the *Bhagavad Gita*) are the heart of the matter, framed and illustrated by the plot; as Narayan puts it, "In a sense, these could be termed 'asides,' but no reader of *The Mahabharata* would miss any part of it." To cut these "asides" would be like cutting all the arias out of a Verdi opera to make it easier to follow the action of the plot. Narayan brilliantly integrates all the levels of the text, constantly enriching the central plot with an awareness of its mythological and philosophical resonances. Right at the beginning, he tells the tangled tale of the ancestry of the heroes by concentrating on the supernatural intervention of the river Ganges and the subsequent employment of gods as biological parents of the sons of the impotent king Pandu—the five legitimate Pandavas and the illegitimate Karna, the dark, tragic figure of the *Mahabharata*.

Narayan claims to be translating the Sanskrit version of the text, and for the most part he does, though he spells the names of some characters as they would have been familiar to him from his Tamil-speaking childhood rather than from the Sanskrit text

(Kunthi instead of Kunti, Satyavathi for Satyavati, etc.). But occasionally he reworks the Sanskrit version of a story in ways that reflect the uneasiness of the later tradition, its inability, or unwillingness, to deal with some of the less admirable attitudes of the ancient text. For instance, there is an episode in which the enemies of the Pandavas plan to kill them (and their mother) by trapping them all in a highly flammable house and setting fire to it; the Pandavas, learning of this plot in advance, dig a tunnel through which they will escape when the fire is set. In the Sanskrit text, they invite a low-caste tribal woman and her five sons to the house, get them drunk, and leave them there when they set the fire and escape through the tunnel, so that their enemies find the six corpses and think that the Pandavas have perished in the fire. The total indifference to the fate of the low-caste tribals on the part of the Pandavas—and, indeed, on the part of the narrator of the text—has become, in recent years, a point of embarrassment to contemporary Hindus sensitive to the injustices of the caste system. In Narayan's retelling, the only person the Pandavas purposely trap in the house is the wicked architect who designed it to kill them; yet afterward people think the Pandavas perished because "the charred remains of a woman and her five sons had been discovered," and we never learn anything more about how those six people got there. Here, and elsewhere, Narayan nimbly sidesteps some of the more controversial social issues.

Another delicate point in the story is the fact that the princess Draupadi is married to all five of the Pandavas; Hindu culture at that time allowed a man to have many wives, but a woman could have only one husband. The Sanskrit text justifies this irregularity at first by saying that, when Arjuna (one of the five brothers) won Draupadi in a contest and returned home with her and with his brothers, he announced to his mother, "Look what we found!" and, without looking up, she replied, like any mother, "Share it among you." Not satisfied with this rather thin excuse, the Sanskrit text goes on to say that all five Pandavas are really incarnations of the god Indra, and Draupadi the incarnation of the goddess of Prosperity, Indra's wife. And then it offers a third explanation:

> The daughter of a great sage longed in vain for a husband; she pleased the god Shiva, who offered her a boon, and she asked for a virtuous husband. But she asked again and again, five times, and so Shiva said, "You will have *five* virtuous husbands." She objected, saying that it is against the law for a woman to have more than one husband, for then there would be promiscuity; moreover, her one husband should have her as a virgin. But Shiva reassured her that a woman is purified every month with her menses and therefore there would be no lapse from *dharma* in her case, since she had asked repeatedly for a husband. Then she asked him if she could be a virgin again for each act of sexual union, and he granted this, too. [1.189.42–8]

When Narayan comes to this sensitive point, he subtly strengthens the first argument by having Arjuna say ("wanting to sound lighthearted"), "Mother, come out, see what bhiksha we have brought today"—thus making Arjuna in part responsible for the misunderstanding by misrepresenting his wife as *bhiksha*, alms won by begging. But Narayan, like the Sanskrit text, also reaches for a stronger justification, and, omitting the second excuse (the five incarnations of Indra), strengthens the third excuse by telling, in place of the tale of the impatient virgin, a story that is not a part of the Sanskrit tradition at all but a well-known Tamil story as well as the subject of a 1936 Tamil film, *Nalayani.* Narayan's version occupies two full pages, but could be summarized thus:

> Draupadi in her previous life was called Nalayani and was married to a cantankerous, leprous sage named Moudgalya. She was utterly devoted to him for many years. One day he told her that he was in fact young and handsome and well, but had assumed his leprous form to test her; and now he would grant her any boon. She asked him to make love to her as five men in five forms; he did, and they spent years in blissful union.

> She never tired of it, but he did; he told her of his intention to retire into loneliness and introspection. Still unsatisfied, she begged Shiva for a husband, over and over, and so he granted her five husbands.

In fact, Narayan leaves out the more lurid details of some versions of the Tamil story, such as the one in which, one day, one of Moudgalya's leprous fingers falls off into her food, and Nalayani continues eating the rice without displaying any revulsion. In Narayan's version, Shiva does not appear, and in place of the god's boon the sage *curses* Nalayani to have, in her next life, five husbands to quench her desire. Just as the Sanskrit text cobbled together three different justifications of Draupadi's polyandry, so Narayan picks from his knowledge of several more Tamil versions the two that best suit his own vision of the text.

That vision is limited to events in which the Pandavas appear, but it does include some of the episodes that might be listed among the disposable mythological and philosophical "asides"—as long as they involve the central characters. Thus Narayan devotes two pages to a summary of the *Bhagavad Gita*, because it is a conversation between Arjuna and the incarnate god Krishna. And he includes five pages of the famous metaphysical riddles of a goblin, because Yudhishthira, the eldest of the five Pandavas, is the one the goblin tests. When the goblin asks, "What is the greatest mystery?" Yudhishthira replies, "Day after day and hour after hour, people die and corpses are carried along, yet the onlookers never realise that they are also to die one day, but think they will live for ever. This is the greatest wonder of the world."

Narayan's telling follows the Sanskrit text in treating Krishna as a mortal prince who is nevertheless, at times, clearly aware of his divinity, such as in the *Bhagavad Gita*. Krishna shifts back and forth between divinity and mortality in the Sanskrit text, and Narayan captures this ambiguity beautifully. When Krishna is sent to the enemy camp to make a final attempt to avoid the Armageddon that does, in fact, take place, he behaves like a mortal prince and is treated like one; Yudhishthira expresses concern for his safety: "I feel nervous to let you go into their midst. They may harm you." But then Narayan adds, "Krishna, who was, after all, a god and confident of himself, said, 'Don't worry about me.'" When Krishna sets out, the weather is literally ominous: thunder comes out of a clear sky, rivers reverse their direction, trees are uprooted. But Narayan remarks, "However, where Krishna's chariot passed, flowers showered down and a gentle cool breeze blew." He selects the precise details to keep the mortal/immortal tension in Krishna alive throughout the book.

Narayan tells the stories so well because they're all his stories, like the tale of Nalayani, stories he never heard for the first time (to use Ramanujan's criterion). He doesn't have to look them up in a book. And he tells them well because he is a novelist of the first water. He is what William Butler Yeats, who translated the ten principal Upanishads with Shree Purohit Swami in 1938, might have been had he also known Sanskrit. Narayan really does know the texts, and the scholarship of the texts, and at the same time he is such a fine novelist, such a great storyteller. He is the ideal person to tell this great story.

Wendy Doniger

Mircea Eliade Distinguished Service Professor of the
History of Religions in the Divinity School; also in the
Department of South Asian Languages and Civilizations,
the Committee on Social Thought, and the College

UNIVERSITY OF CHICAGO, OCTOBER 2012

INTRODUCTION

THE ORIGINAL COMPOSITION in the Sanskrit language runs to one hundred thousand stanzas in verse, thus making it the longest composition in the world: in sheer quantity eight times longer than *The Iliad* and *The Odyssey* put together. A great deal of scholarly research, based on internal evidence, cross references, and astronomical data occurring incidentally in the texts, has gone on for years in order to reach a conclusion in regard to the authorship and date of this epic. There can, however, be no such thing as a final statement on the subject. However, a few salient points have emerged from all the research.

The nucleus of the story in some form, perhaps a ballad, was known in 1500 B.C. The tension between two branches of a ruling family of the warrior caste, the ups and downs in their fortunes, and a mighty battle that ensued to settle the question of supremacy were familiar facts long before the Christian Era. The geographical locations, such as Hastinapura and Kurukshetra, are still extant in the northernmost part of India. Commemorative festivals are still being celebrated there in certain seasons, associated with the characters in the tale. "The Pandavas were exiled here . . ." or ". . . lived in these forests . . ." and so forth.

This tale of heroism, persecution, and intrigue must have passed into ballads or similar modes of popular entertainment. Out of these the first version of the epic was composed, consisting of twenty-four thousand stanzas, the authorship being attributed to Vyasa. Now, once again, speculation and doubt begins to grow around the name "Vyasa". While ninety-nine percent of our public would accept the name and venerate him without question as an immortal, inspired sage, research-minded scholars have their own doubts and speculations. They explain that "Vyasa" could be a generic title, and that there could have been at different stages of the epic's life several others who must have assumed the name for the purpose of composition. Speaking for myself, I would rather accept the traditional accounts. The conclusions of cold, factual research seem like "catching the rainbow with one's fingers," to quote a line from the epic itself.

Vyasa's epic was originally entitled *Jaya,* which means triumph or victory. When the vision of it came to him through the grace of Brahma, the Creator, Vyasa needed someone to take it down as he recited it. Ganesha, the god with an elephant head, accepted the assignment on one condition—that there should be no pause in the dictation. The author accepted this condition, provided that Ganesha realized and understood the meaning of every word before putting it down in writing.

Vyasa kept up his dictation at a breathless speed, and Ganesha took it down with matching zest. When, at one point, his stylus failed, he broke off one of his tusks and continued the writing. The composer, whenever he found his amanuensis outrunning him, checked his speed by composing, here and there, passages—terse, packed and concentrated—which would force him to pause to get at the meaning. There are thus several passages in *The Mahabharata* which convey layers of meaning depending upon the stress and syllabification while reciting them aloud.

Jaya became *Bharata* at the next stage, when Vysampayana, who had listened to the original narrative from Vyasa himself, conveyed it to an assembly of listeners at the court of Janamejaya. The work acquired considerable volume at this stage, swollen to about fifty thousand stanzas.

Much later, it was narrated again at another assembly of sages in a forest, this time by one Sauti, who had heard it at Janamejaya's court.

Sauti is a great traveller and arrives at the ashram of a sage named Saunaka, set in deep woods, where a number of sages are gathered reposefully after a prolonged performance of certain rites and sacrifices for the welfare of humanity. While they are resting thus, Sauti walks in—a wayfarer. As prescribed by the code of hospitality, the sages offer him shelter and rest, and seat him comfortably. When the formalities are over, and when they feel certain that their guest has rested and overcome the fatigue of travel, they ask, "O guest, where are you coming from? What strange and rare experiences have you undergone and what places and men have you seen?"

Sauti answers, "I visited the holy land of Kurukshetra where was fought the eighteen-day war between the Pandavas and their cousins, the Kauravas, and where the ground was washed in blood. I visited it after I had heard the tale narrated by Vysampayana at the great Serpent Sacrifice* performed at Janamejaya's court." And Sauti's narrative acquired further quantity and quality at this stage.

At other unspecified times, additions were made by each narrator. Episodes, philosophies, and moral lessons were added until the epic came to its present length of one hundred thousand stanzas. In this form, about A.D. 400, it came to be known as *The Mahabharata*, *maha* being a prefix indicating greatness.

---

* King Parikshit, who became the ruler of Hastinapura after the Pandavas, was cursed to die of a snakebite for playing mischief on a hermit, who was in deep meditation. On the fulfilment of this curse, Parikshit's son, Janamejaya performed a sacrifice, in revenge, which caused the extinction of all the snakes on earth. At this sacrifice Vysampayana narrates the story of *The Mahabharata* as he had heard it from Vyasa himself.

Incidentally, we may note that with the introduction of Parikshit as a successor to the Pandavas, Vyasa composed a fresh narrative called *The Bhagavata*, which has almost the stature of an epic.

Scholars have worked hard to identify the recensions, alterations, and additions, and definitive editions are available indicating the changes from the original versions. It is a controversial field, but the main story is accepted on all hands and beyond all argument: once upon a time in ancient Hastinapura lived a royal family—with five brothers of divine origin on one side, and their one hundred cousins on the other, at war with each other. This framework is filled with details and lines of the finest poetic values in Sanskrit. Of its literary and other values, here is a summary as the author himself declared it:

When Vyasa had the epic all complete in his mind, he invoked Brahma, the Creator, and explained, "I have composed a poem which is vast. Therein are revealed the mystery and the subtleties of the Vedas and Upanishads; descriptions of creeds and modes of life; the history of past, present, and future; rules for the four castes; the essence of the Puranas, of asceticism, and rules for the acolyte; the dimensions of the sun, moon, and stars; a description of the four yugas; a definition of charity, the subject of the incarnation of souls for specific purposes; the sciences and the healing of sickness; also a description of places of pilgrimage, of rivers, mountains, and forests, and of heavenly cities and palaces; the art of war; descriptions of different nations, their languages, and their qualities; and of the all-pervading universal spirit." And at this stage Brahma said, "Call on Ganesha. He is the one fittest to take down your poem as you recite it."

The Mahabharata consists of eighteen parvas (or parts), as many volumes by the present measure of production. Being a work dependent on oral report, there is naturally much repetition, perhaps for the benefit of a listener who might have missed a piece, as the narration goes on day after day. In this method of narrative a character reporting elsewhere on a situation which the reader already knows, gives again a complete account to his listener. The epic form is detailed and leisurely, and the technique of narration is different from what we are used to. There is an unhurrying quality about it which gives it stature. To point a moral, a complete, independent story of great length and detail may be included, a deviation from the mainstream which can run to several hundred pages. Thus, we have in *The Mahabharata* the well-known legends such as Harischandra, Nala, and Savitri, Yayati, Draupadi (presented here in an adapted form), Shakuntala, and Sibi, which are included in my previous book, *Gods, Demons, and Others.*

Another factor which swells *The Mahabharata* is philosophic discussion—discourses on life and conduct which one or another of the sages expounds—sometimes running to several hundred lines at a time. *The Bhagavad Gita* is an instance of such a situation. When the opposing armies are ready to attack each other, Krishna reveals and elaborates (in eighteen chapters) the *Gita* philosophy.

Great edicts in the text often center round the duties of a king or a commoner. Thus we have a whole parva, or part, called *Santhi,* a full volume in which Bhishma, while dying, discourses on the duties of a king for the benefit of Yudhistira. This is followed by *Anusasana,* another complete book, which is equally voluminous, detailing the importance of rituals, worship, and their proper performance. In a sense, these could be termed "asides," but no reader of *The Mahabharata* in India would miss any part of it.

Although this epic is a treasure house of varied interests, my own preference is the story. It is a great tale with well-defined characters who talk and act with robustness and zest—heroes and villains, saints and kings, women of beauty, all displaying great human qualities, super-human endurance, depths of sinister qualities as well as power, satanic hates and intrigues—all presented against an impressive background of ancient royal capitals, forests, and mountains.

The actual physical quantum of the epic is staggering. If only a single word could be used to indicate the gist of each stanza, the total length of such a sampling would still run to one hundred thousand words. I have omitted none of the episodes relevant to the destinies of the chief characters. I have kept myself to the mainstream and held my version within readable limits.

For a modern reader in English, one has necessarily to select and condense. I have not attempted any translation, as it is impossible to convey in English the rhythm and depth of the original language. The very sound of Sanskrit has a hypnotic quality which is inevitably lost in translation. One has to feel content with a prose narrative in story form.

For me, the special interest in this work is the role the author himself plays in the story. Vyasa not only composed the narrative, but being aware of the past and future of all his characters, helps them with solutions when they find themselves in a dilemma. Sometimes he may see into the future and emphasize the inevitability of certain coming events, making his heroes resign themselves to their fate.

In this way, at a moment when the Pandavas are all happily settled at Indraprastha, Vyasa hints to Yudhistira that he will be the total destroyer of their clan and race thirteen years hence. Yudhistira accepts this news with terror and resignation, stating, "We cannot change the circumstances that destiny decrees. But I shall do nothing to provoke anyone in any manner and practise absolute non-violence in thought, word and deed. It is the only way to meet the decrees of Fate." This episode comes long before the gambling match which leads to the Pandavas' ruin. When the invitation to gamble comes, Yudhistira accepts it, in addition to his own partiality for the game, as a part of his policy not to displease others. When others argue fiercely with him on any matter, he always answers them with gentleness and calm.

Earlier in the story, when the Pandavas wander without

aim, they are directed by Vyasa to go to Ekavrata and then on to Panchala, where they are destined to find their bride. Throughout, the author lives with his characters, and this is the greatest charm of this work for me. Vyasa's birth itself is explained at the beginning of the epic. He was conceived in a ferry by his virgin mother, who later begot by Santanu the two brothers, the widows of the younger brother becoming pregnant through Vyasa's grace, and giving birth to Dhritarashtra and Pandu, whose sons in turn become the chief figures of *The Mahabharata.*

R. K. NARAYAN
Mysore, 1977

LIST OF CHARACTERS AND PLACES OF ACTION IN THE STORY

(If not otherwise indicated, the "a" is broad, as in "ah"; the "th" is a soft "t" as in "thyme"; the "u" is "oo" as in "cool"; the "i" is "ee" as in "seen.")

AGNI (ag′ nee): God of Fire.
AMBA (am′ ba): Princess, sister of Ambika and Ambalika, who was transformed into Sikandi, a male warrior.
AMBALIKA (am ba′ lee ka): wife of Vichitravirya.
AMBIKA (am′ bee ka): wife of Vichitravirya.
ARJUNA (ar′ joo na): third son of Kunthi.
ASWATHAMA (as wat ta′ ma): son of Drona.
ASWINS (as′ wins): twins, minor gods.
BAKASURA (ba ka′ soo ra): a demon.
BHARADWAJ (ba ra dwaj′): a sage, father of Drona.
BHIMA (bee′ ma): second son of Kunthi.
BHIMASENA (bee′ ma say′ na): same as Bhima.
BHISHMA (beesh′ ma): Devavratha's later name.
BRIHANNALA (bri ha′ na la): Arjuna's assumed name in Virata.
CHITRANGADA (chee tran′ ga da): son of Santanu by Satyavathi.
DEVAVRATHA (day va′ vra ta): son of Santanu.
DHANANJAYA (da nan′ ja ya): another name for Arjuna.
DHARMARAJA (dar ma ra′ ja): Yudhistira.
DHAUMYA (dowm′ ya): Yudhistira's chief priest.
DHRISHTADYUMNA (dri′ shta dyoom′ na): son of Drupada.
DHRITARASHTRA (dri ta rash′ tra): son of Ambika and Ambalika through Vyasa.

DHURVASA (door va′ sa): a sage known for his quick temper.
DRAUPADI (drow′ pa dee): wife of the Pandava brothers; also called Panchali or Yajnaseni.
DRONA (dro′ na): a teacher of military science and art to the sons and nephews of Dhritarashtra.
DRUPADA (droo′ pa da): King of Panchala.
DUSSASANA (doo sa′ sa na): second son of Dhritarashtra.
DURYODHANA (door yo′ da na): eldest son of Dhritarashtra.
DWAITA (dwi′ ta)
DWARAKA (dwa′ ra ka)
EKAVRATA (ay ka′ vra ta)
GANDHARI (gan da′ ree): wife of Dhritarashtra.
GANGA (gan′ ga): Santanu's first wife.
GHATOTKACHA (ga tot′ ka cha): Bhima's demon son.
HARI (ha′ ree): one of Krishna's names.
HASTINAPURA (ha stee na′ poo ra)
INDRA (een′ dra): Chief of the Gods.
INDRAPRASTHA (een′ dra pra' sta)
JANAMEJAYA (ja na ma jay′ ya): son of King Parikshit.
JAYADRATHA (ja ya′ dra ta): ruler of Sindu, and son-in-law of Dhritarashtra.
KAMYAKA (kam′ ya ka)
KARNA (kar′ na): son of Kunthi before she married Pandu.
KHANDAVAPRASTHA (kan′ da va pra′ sta)
KICHAKA (kee′ cha ka): General of Virata's army and brother of the Queen.
KRIPA (kri′ pa): another guru of the young men at the court of Dhritarashtra.
KRISHNA (kreesh′ na): eighth incarnation of Vishnu.
KUNTHI (koon′ tee): wife of Pandu.
KURUKSHETRA (koo ru kshay′ tra)
MADRI (ma′ dree): wife of Pandu.
MATSYA (mat′ sya)
NAKULA (na′ koo la): one of the twins born to Madri.
NARADA (na′ ra da): a sage constantly on the move between all the worlds.

PANCHALA (pan cha′ la)

PANCHALI (pan cha′ lee): Draupadi or Yajnaseni; wife of the Pandava brothers.

PANDAVA (pan′ da va): generic title of the five brothers, sons of Pandu.

PANDU (pan′ doo): son of Ambika and Ambalika through Vyasa.

PARASAR (pa ra′ sar): a sage who begot Vyasa through Satyavathi before she married Santanu.

PARIKSHIT (pa ree′ ksheet): successor of Yudhistira and son of Abhimanyu.

PARTHA (par′ ta): another name for Arjuna.

PARISHTA (pa ree′ shta): a king, father of Drupada.

PUROCHANA (poo ro′ cha na): an architect in the service of Duryodhana.

RADHE (ra′ day): foster-mother of Karna.

SAHADEVA (sa ha day′ va): one of the twins born to Madri.

SAKUNI (sa′ koo nee): uncle of Duryodhana.

SALYA (sal′ ya): a king, father of Madri, the second wife of Pandu.

SANJAYA (san′ ja ya): a commentator and a companion of Dhritarashtra.

SANTANU (san′ ta noo): King of Hastinapura.

SATYAKI (sat′ ya kee): Krishna's companion and charioteer, and supporter of Pandavas.

SATYAVATHI (sat ya′ va tee): daughter of a fisherman, second wife of King Santanu.

SAUTI (sow′ tee): narrator.

SIKANDI (see kan′ dee): Amba.

SURYA (soor′ ya): the Sun God.

SUSURMAN (soo soor′ man): King of Trigarta.

SUVALA (soo′ va la): another name for Sakuni.

UPAPLAVYA (oo pa′ pla vya)

UTTARA (oot′ ta ra): son of Virata.

UTTARAI (oot′ ta ri): daughter of Virata; wife of Abhimanyu, the son of Arjuna.

VARUNA (va roo′ na): God of Rain.

VARANAVATTA (va′ ra na vat′ ta)

VAYU (va′ yoo): God of Wind and Energy.

VASISHTA (va see′ shta): a sage.

VICHITRAVIRYA (vee chee′ tra veer′ ya): son of Santanu by Satyavathi.

VIDURA (vee′ doo ra): son of Ambika and Ambalika through Vyasa.

VIKARNA (vee kar′ na): Dhritarashtra's son, who crossed over to the Pandava camp.

VIRATA (vee ra′ ta): King of Matsya.

VISHNU (veesh′ noo): the Supreme God.

VYASA (vya′ sa): son of Parasar and composer of *The Mahabharata*.

VYSAMPAYANA (vi sam pa′ ya na): narrator.

YAJNASENI (ya gya say′ nee)

YAMA (ya′ ma): God of Death and Justice.

YUDHISTIRA (yoo dee′ stee ra): eldest son of Kunthi.

GENERATION TREE

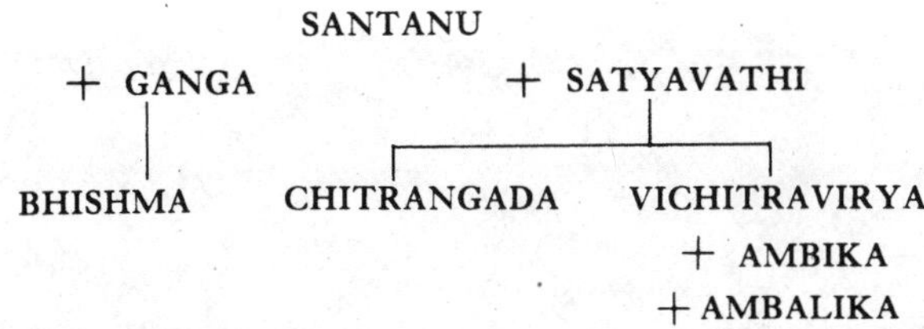

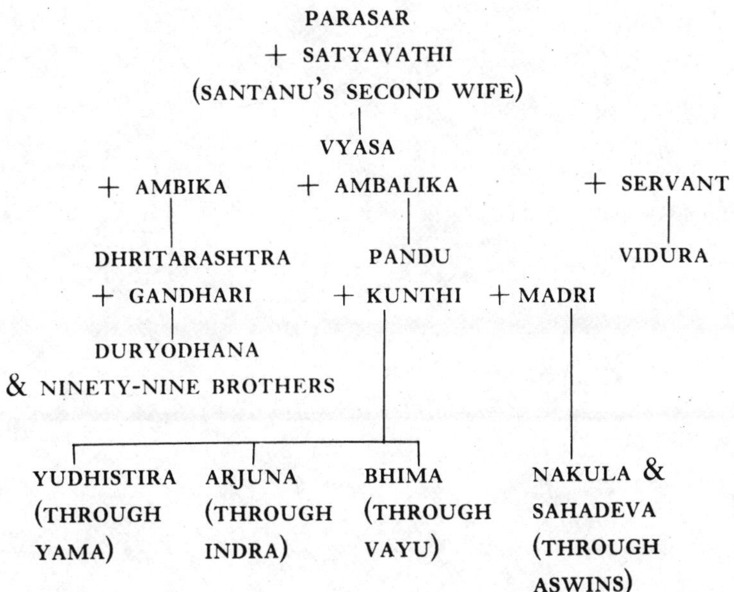

This work opens the eyes of the world blinded by ignorance. As the sun dispels darkness, so does Bharata by its exposition of religion, duty, action, contemplation, and so forth. As the full moon by shedding soft light helps the buds of the lotus to open, so this Purana by its exposition expands the human intellect. The lamp of history illumines the 'whole mansion of the womb of Nature.'

—Vyasa

The Mahabharata

1 The Eighth Baby

SANTANU WAS THE RULER of an ancient kingdom with its capital at Hastinapura*. One day while out hunting, he came upon a lovely maiden by the river and fell in love with her. He announced himself and asked, "Will you be my wife?" Being equally attracted to him, she said, "Yes, but listen carefully to what I say now. When I am married, I must be absolutely free to do what I like. At no stage should you ever question my action. I'll stay as your wife only as long as you observe this rule." Santanu accepted the condition wholeheartedly and they were married.

In due course, she brought forth a baby, and as soon as it could be lifted, drowned it in the river. Santanu was shocked and bewildered, but could ask no questions. The next child

* In the present-day geographical context, this is in the state of Uttar Pradesh, about 100 kilometers northeast of Delhi.

was also promptly drowned, and then another and another. As soon as it was born, she carried off every child to the river and returned to the palace with a smile of satisfaction. Her husband never referred to this monstrous habit of hers for fear that she might leave, since in all other respects she proved a splendid wife.

When the eighth child came and she got ready to dispose of it, he followed her. Unable to control himself any more, he cried, "This is too horrible. Stop it!"

She replied calmly, "Yes, I will spare this child, but the moment has come for us to part."

"Oh, tell me why, before you go."

So she explained, "Know me now as Ganga, the deity of this river. I took human form only in order to give birth to these eight babies, as ordained. I married you because you were the only one worthy of fathering them. The children are the eight vasus.* In their past life, for the sin of stealing Sage Vasishta's rare cow, Nandini, they were cursed to be born on earth. On appealing, seven of them were permitted to leave their physical bodies soon after birth and return to heaven. However, the eighth member among them, who had arranged the whole expedition to satisfy the whims of his wife, and who had actually stolen the cow—the one I am holding now—is to continue his existence on earth as a man of brilliant accomplishments, but condemned to a life of celibacy."

After these explanations Ganga said, "I'll take this child with me now, but restore him to you later."

His desperate questions, "Oh, when? Where?" were ignored as she vanished with the child into the river.

Years later, once again at the same spot, the King was accosted by Ganga and presented with their son, now grown into a youth. She said, "I have brought him up with care. Now he can go with you. He is named Devavratha. He has

---

* A class of deities, eight in number, attendants of Indra.

mastered all the Vedas under Sage Vasishta himself; he will be a great warrior, an expert in the use of astras, and endowed with rare mental and spiritual qualities. Take him home." At this, she vanished.

King Santanu returned to the palace a very happy man, and installed the youth as the heir apparent.

Four years later, King Santanu, following a deer while hunting, came upon a beautiful maiden in the woods and was once again love-stricken. "Who are you? Why are you here?" he asked.

She answered, "I am the daughter of a fisherman. I help my father to ferry pilgrims across the river."

The King sought her father and asked, "Will you permit us to marry?" He agreed readily but added, "On the condition that the son born to her will be your successor." The King could not accept this and returned to the palace frustrated.

In the days that followed, the young Prince Devavratha, noticing his father's melancholic state, enquired, "What's troubling your mind?"

The King replied, "I am worried about the future, or rather the future of our dynasty. You are my only son. If any mishap befalls you, our dynasty will come to an end. The scriptures say that having an only son is like having no son. You are at all times engaged in the exercise of arms and you will be a great warrior, but how can one prophesy a warrior's end?"

The Prince was bewildered by his father's statement and sought an explanation, privately, from their minister. The minister explained that the King desired to marry the fisherman's daughter, but that he felt unable to accept the man's condition. Devavratha visited the fisherman at his hut and assured him that when the time came, his daughter's issue would succeed to the throne. The fisherman, being too farsighted, had a further misgiving, and asked, "Who will be my grandson's successor?"

"Well, naturally, his son," said Devavratha. "Perhaps you fear that if I marry, my sons will be rivals to your daughter's progeny. I hereby promise that I'll live and die a bachelor. This is a firm vow."

The fisherman was pleased. Devavratha—who from that time came to be known as *Bhishma,* meaning "one of firm vow"—addressed the girl, "Now get into the chariot, please. You will be my mother henceforth."

Satyavathi, the daughter of the fisherman, bore the King two sons, Chitrangada and Vichitravirya. Chitrangada succeeded Santanu, but he was killed in a battle with a gandharva king. His brother, Vichitravirya, who was still young, was installed as his successor, with Bhishma acting as a regent at the request of Satyavathi herself.

Bhishma, anxious not to let the family become extinct, waited for a chance to find a bride for his ward. When the ruler of Kasi announced a swayamwara for his three daughters named Amba, Ambika, and Ambalika, he presented himself at that court, where many princes from far and near had assembled to catch the eye of the beauties. At a crucial moment, Bhishma rose and announced, "Of the several forms of choosing a bride, as the sages have mentioned, the noblest is that in which a maiden is acquired by force from amidst a valiant gathering such as this." Thus saying, he seized the three girls before anyone could understand what was happening and, pushing them into his chariot, sped away, pursued by the outraged princes and the father of the girls. He fought his pursuers off and arrived at Hastinapura with the girls intended for his half-brother, Vichitravirya.

When the date for their wedding was settled, the eldest of the sisters, called Amba, said, "I cannot marry your brother, as my heart is already set on the King of Salwa and I cannot consider anyone else."

Bhishma admitted her objection and sent her away to

Salwa as she desired.* Ambika and Ambalika were married to Vichitravirya and they lived a happy life for seven years, when Vichitravirya contracted a wasting disease and died without issue.

At this, Satyavathi pleaded with Bhishma, "Under certain circumstances, one could perpetuate one's line through the widows of one's brother. The shastras permit it. Please save these girls from ending their lives as barren women. Our race should continue."

Bhishma replied, "Order me to do anything else, I will obey you. I cannot break my vow of celibacy."

Satyavathi sounded desperate as she said, "There will be no one to offer our ancestors the funeral cake, no one to perform their annual ceremonies on the days of remembrance. Save our ancestors. By your good deeds, you must help them attain their proper regions in the next world. I'm your mother; you must obey my order. Raise children on these two lovely daughters-in-law of mine. Ascend the throne yourself and rule Hastinapura. It rests upon you now to see that the Kuru** clan does not perish at this point. You owe a duty to our ancestors and to the future generations."

"No, no, no," Bhishma cried. "I cannot violate any of my vows, even if you sanction it. You must think of some other means."

Satyavathi just repeated, "You are adamant. It will be a great solace to those two girls, now plunged in sorrow, to have children."

Bhishma said, "Once a vow is made, it's eternal. It cannot

---

* Salwa rejected Amba. When she came back to Bhishma and offered to marry him, he refused her owing to his vow and sent her back to Salwa, who rejected her again. So back and forth she was shuttled. Amba became desperate and, holding Bhishma responsible for all her humiliations and sufferings, she vowed, after a final appeal to him, to kill him. Her transformation into a male warrior named Sikandi, who was responsible for Bhishma's end, is explained elsewhere.

** "Kurus" and "Kauravas" sometimes seem to be interchangeable terms in the original text, but "Kauravas" specifically indicates Duryodhana and his brothers, while "Kurus" indicates both the Kauravas and the Pandavas.

be modified or given up. There must be other remedies. Let us think it over."

After further consideration, another proposal occurred to Satyavathi. She turned to Bhishma, "Now listen to this story and tell me if it seems proper to you. Years ago, I was in the habit of ferrying people across the river and once my passenger happened to be an eminent rishi, Parasar. When I was rowing him across, he looked passionately at me and spoke words of love, whereupon I trembled with fear. I was afraid of being cursed by him if I repulsed his advances, and of my father's fury if ever he should come to know of any misconduct on my part. I pleaded with the sage, 'I was born of a fish mother and an odour of fish always clings to me.'

" 'I am aware of your origin,' he said, 'how you came to be conceived in the womb of a fish. Your real father was a gandharva who, while flying across the river, spilled his seed, which entered the fish while it was looking up. Thus you were conceived and, when born, the fisherman adopted you. The odour of fish clings to you because of your origin, but I will dispel it.' By his magical powers, he not only rid me of my lifelong fish odour, but endowed my person with a perpetual fragrance!"

"Yes, my father told me that the first time he was drawn by a fragrance pervading the woods, and following it, reached you."

"In return for this favour, I surrendered to the sage's embraces, the rishi having caused a fog to arise and envelop us so that we might remain unobserved. The rishi said, 'Stay on that island and give birth to your child; thereby your virginity will not be considered lost.' Thus was Vyasa born. He is a sage and a savant, and I have his promise to come to me when I need him. I can summon him by thought. In a sense and as a matter of fact, he is my eldest son. If you approve, I will summon him."

Bhishma replied, "You know best."

She thought of Vyasa and he arrived at once. Satyavathi

explained their predicament to him and begged him to perpetuate their race through her daughters-in-law. He agreed, but asked for a year's time to make himself presentable, as he was going through a period of penance and was hardly in a state to approach women. But Satyavathi brushed aside his reservations and left him no choice in the matter.

Vyasa ordered, "Let the girls be prepared; I will come back."

Satyavathi directed her first daughter-in-law, Ambika, to dress and decorate herself and wait in her bedchamber. When Vyasa came to her, the girl was repelled by his appearance, clothes, complexion, hirsuteness, and uncleanliness. She went to bed with him with her eyes tightly shut.

Subsequently, Vyasa declared to Satyavathi, "A beautiful child will be born to Ambika. He'll rule this country, but he will be blind since Ambika shut her eyes during conception."

Thereupon Satyavathi induced him to come again and offered him her second daughter-in-law, Ambalika. The girl, decorated and dressed, waited in bed, but at the approach of Vyasa, she turned pale with fright.

Vyasa told Satyavathi later, "The child born to Ambalika will be brave and distinguished but will be pallid."

Satyavathi persuaded Ambalika to give herself another chance after begging Vyasa to make a third visit. When Vyasa arrived, Ambalika dressed her maidservant appropriately and substituted her in her bed. The servant was bold and responsive, which pleased Vyasa, and hence the child born of this union was normal.

The eldest son, blind from birth, was named Dhritarashtra. The second, owing to his pallor, was named Pandu; and the third child born to the servant maid, who was normal in every way, was named Vidura, whose wisdom, judgement, and courage in speech and action, have made him an outstanding character in the story of *The Mahabharata*, which may be said to begin with these three personalities.

Dhritarashtra grew up under the care of Bhishma, who found him a suitable bride when he attained manhood—the Princess of Gandhara, called Gandhari. In order to share her husband's blind condition, she spent the rest of her life with eyes bandaged tight. However, owing to his handicap, Dhritarashtra surrendered his authority to his younger brother, Pandu, who had two wives called Kunthi and Madri.

Pandu's enthronement received all-round approval. He proved to be valorous and just, and enhanced the prestige and power of the Kuru clan by subjugating their neighbouring kingdoms. After these martial exertions, Pandu sought relaxation in a retreat amidst a forest of Sal trees on the southern slopes of the Himalayas.

One day while hunting, Pandu killed a deer, which was engaged in love play with its mate. Before dying, the deer—actually a celestial being—uttered the curse, "Your end will come at a moment when you attempt to unite with your wife." Thus was an irrevocable celibacy imposed upon Pandu. He became unhappy and planned to renounce the world. To die without issue, never to approach his wives again, seemed terrible.

At this juncture, Kunthi explained to him a blessing conferred on her by Sage Dhurvasa when she was young. Dhurvasa was a quick-tempered man, but Kunthi managed to please him by her ministrations when he visited her parents. He blessed her, "May you be the mother of godly children," and taught her a mantra with which she could invoke any god of her choice and enjoy his company. Dhurvasa had a seer's vision and realised that she would need this help in the future. After he left, she became curious about the privilege conferred on her, and invoked Surya, the Sun God, by uttering the mantra. He stood before her in all his glory and asked, "What is your desire?"

"No, no, nothing," she stammered. "I was only . . . playing. . . ." She prostrated herself before him and begged, "Forgive me, please go, forgive me."

"Did you not know that you should not play thus; and that a mantra is not to be trifled with?"

She stood speechless, petrified with fear, whereupon the god took her in his arms and caressed her and left after a prolonged dalliance. A child was born of this union, his future indicated by the fact that he was born encased in armour and wearing large earrings. The child was named Karna.

To avoid a scandal, Kunthi placed the baby in a basket and floated it down the river. It was picked up by one Radhe, the wife of a charioteer, who dwelt on the river bank. The foundling was viewed as a godsend and cherished by the couple.

On hearing this story, Pandu said, "The gods have blessed you thus for fulfilling a divine purpose. The curse on me debars fatherhood for the rest of my life. But you could be a unique and blessed mother. Don't let time run out. Prepare yourself to invite and receive the gods. First pray to Yama, the God of Death and Ultimate Justice. He is the most judicious among the celestial beings. The son born to him will always lead our Kuru race along the right path at all times."

Kunthi prepared herself in her chambers, meditated upon Yama, and uttered the mantra which she had already experimented with. Yama responded to her invocation, and this being her second effort, she knew how to conduct herself before a god. Thus came her first born. A heavenly voice announced at the time of his birth, "The child will be the best of men, truthful in thought, word, and deed, and also blessed with strength and courage. He shall be named Yudhistira, which means one unflinching in war."

Pandu induced Kunthi to pray for a second son. "A kshatriya's life cannot be complete, except with possession of physical strength. So now pray for a son endowed with extraordinary strength." Kunthi invoked Vayu, the God of Wind, and got a child so strong that when he rolled off his mother's side he caused a minor earthquake. The child was named Bhimasena.

After this Pandu once again thought, "We must have a warrior in our family whose prowess at arms should be unmatched." After a full year's penance observed by both himself and Kunthi, they prayed to Indra, the Chief of Gods, who had great endowments. When Kunthi gave birth to a son, a heavenly voice said, "This son will be unmatched in energy, wisdom, and the knowledge of weapons; he will wield with ease every kind of weapon and subjugate all his enemies and bring fame to the race of Kurus." This child was named Arjuna.

After this Kunthi declined to bear any more children, although Pandu was eager for more. Madri, his second wife, also pleaded at this time that she should not be left barren, while Kunthi had three children. Pandu appealed to Kunthi to impart the mantra to Madri. Invoking the gods Aswins, she conceived and brought forth the brilliant twins Nakula and Sahadeva. These five brothers came to be known as the Pandavas.

Meanwhile, Gandhari had borne a hundred sons by Dhritarashtra, the blind King, the eldest being Duryodhana, the second Dussasana, and so on. These set themselves up as enemies of the Pandavas all their life, and *The Mahabharata* may be said to be a tale of conflict between the two groups that never ceased except with death.

Pandu's end came on rather suddenly. One day, going into the woods in the company of Madri, he was overcome by the spirit of the hour and the mood of the spring, with tender leaves on the trees, and colourful blossoms, and the cries of birds, and the stirrings of animal life all around. Unable to resist the attraction of Madri at his side, he seized her passionately, in spite of her reminder of the curse, and died during intercourse. Entrusting her twins to the care of Kunthi, Madri ascended the funeral pyre along with her husband and ended her life.

2 Enter—the Players

FROM THE SYLVAN RETREAT where Pandu had spent his later days, after his death, Kunthi came to Hastinapura with her five children to live under the care of Dhritarashtra and Bhishma. Dhritarashtra, at this stage at least, treated alike the one hundred sons born to his wife and the five of his brother's sons. They were nourished, educated, and trained without partiality.

The children played all day among themselves, but at every game Bhimasena teased and played pranks on his cousins. Duryodhana gradually began to feel irritated when he found himself the butt of these pranks and practical jokes. When he walked or ran, Bhimasena tripped him from behind; when he climbed a tree, Bhima would seize its trunk in his mighty grip and give it a shake till the other fell off his perch. At a later stage, Duryodhana began to feel that existence would be impossible with his cousins around.

Through his accomplices, he made a few attempts to get rid of them, especially Bhima, who was drugged, poisoned, trussed up, and thrown into the river. But Bhima managed to overcome the effect of the drug, neutralised the poison, and floated up from the depths of the river.

When Bhishma appointed a guru to train the young men in the use of arms, Duryodhana noticed with bitterness that the master was paying special attention to Arjuna. The guru, called Drona, was of brahmin origin and, unusually for a brahmin, was an expert in warfare and the science of weapons. He coached his pupils with great sincerity and made them all versatile fighters. He also trained his only son, Aswathama, with special care.

In addition to what he was directly taught, Arjuna watched unseen all those special lessons Aswathama was given by his father and absorbed them also. Arjuna soon became adept in wielding the sword, the mace, and the lance, or in hitting the mark with his arrow, however difficult the target might be. He fought with equal ease on foot, horseback, or chariot; single-handed he could engage a vast number in combat. In addition to these skills, he could effectively send out astras, missiles propelled by mystic incantations. Thus he could perform what seemed miracles with his bow and arrow.

One day, to test his pupils, Drona mounted an artificial eagle on a tall pole and told them to try to sever its head from its body when he gave the order. First he said, "Tell me each of you all that comes within your sight when you take aim." He started with Yudhistira, who explained, "I see you and that tree and the branches. . . ."

Drona shook his head and cried, "Stop, stop; next." The next also gave an account of all that came within the range of his vision. Finally he summoned Arjuna and asked, "What do you see?"

"A bird above."

"How much of it?"

"Only its head."

"What part of the head?"

"The forehead."

"What part of the forehead?"

"The centre."

"Shoot," Drona ordered, and Arjuna brought down the head of the bird neatly. Drona hugged him with joy. "This indeed is marksmanship!"

Arjuna had an occasion to prove again his extraordinary gift. Once, when bathing in the river, Drona's thighs were caught in the jaws of a crocodile. Arjuna immediately shot five arrows into the river and sliced up the monster into fragments. For this service, Drona imparted to him the secret of employing a very special weapon. But he warned him, "If hurled against an inferior foe, it might burn up the entire universe; keep it with care. If you encounter a supernatural foe, you may use it without any thought. With this weapon in your hand, no one in the world can ever conquer you."

Bhima and Duryodhana were experts in wielding the mace for offence and defence. Aswathama was an expert in several branches of arms, the twins in handling the sword. Yudhistira was unexcelled as a chariot fighter (one who could move his chariot for attack and counter-attack in a battle and fight in motion). At last Drona reported to King Dhritarashtra, "Your sons have completed their training. They have nothing more to learn. Now, we must arrange an exhibition of their skills. Let there be a public ceremony, which the citizens may witness."

On a vast ground, galleries and pavilions were built for the spectators around a spacious arena. On a chosen day, invitations were sent out far and wide. The King, along with his wife and members of the royal family, occupied special seats. Many princes from the neighbouring countries were also present. Drona, clad in white, entered the arena and formally announced to the public the names and accomplishments of his pupils, presenting them one by one. A commentator, Sanjaya, sat beside Dhritarashtra and narrated in detail everything he witnessed on the arena. "Now, here they come. Yudhistira enters on horseback, leading the rest. His younger brothers, in the order of their rank and age, are giving a display, each bearing his favourite weapon in hand. It is really wonderful. Ah! The spectators are excited and now you can hear their shouts. Ah, some are averting their heads for fear that the arrows may fall on them, but the arrows fly with such precision that they fall within an inch of those in the front rows. Well done! Well done. . . . What grace and agility! Now their guru approaches each one of them to bless them publicly. He looks so happy . . ." Dhritarashtra listened to this account enthusiastically at first, but later rather coldly asked, "What about my sons? You have said nothing about them."

"Yes, yes, they are there, also resplendent, perhaps waiting for their turn."

"You say nothing about Duryodhana."

"Oh, he is just entering with his mace held high and Bhima faces him, swinging his mace like a wild elephant raising its trunk. . . . Duryodhana is surrounded by all his brothers. He looks like the red planet studded around with stars; his face is flushed with anger and if they clash with their maces it will be an unbearable spectacle. But Aswathama stands upright in the midst of your sons . . . he moves with ease and confidence between the clashing mountains. He has been asked by his father, Drona, to restrain Bhima and your son and separate them.

"Arjuna is at the centre of the stage. . . . Oh, he has mastered the astras, and the mantras that charge them with power. Now with one arrow he has created fire; now water, air, and storm. Don't you hear? Now clouds, now land, he has created mountains around, and now when he employs another weapon, all of them vanish. Now on a chariot, now on foot, so dexterous and fast. Now he discharges twenty shafts into the hollow of a bull horn, suspended overhead and swinging in the wind. Marvellous feats . . . marvellous feats. . . . His master sheds tears of joy. Arjuna pauses only to receive the pat on his back."

Nearly at the close of Arjuna's grand performance, when the public excitement was dying down and the musical instruments became silent, there arose at the gate a sudden uproar. A warrior, hitherto unnoticed, clad in a mail coat, brilliant looking and wearing earrings, stood throwing challenges in a thundering tone. It was Karna, whom no one had seen before except Kunthi, when she had floated him down the river as an infant. Being the offspring of the Sun God, he had a radiant personality, and people began to look at each other and ask, "Who is this youth? Who is this?"

The warrior threw a casual, indifferent salute in the direction of Drona and the other elders and proclaimed, "I can do all that Partha* has done and more." With Drona's permission, he repeated every act that Arjuna had performed. This delighted Duryodhana, who hugged him, happy at finding a rival to Arjuna, and promised, "Your wish will be fulfilled whatever it may be. Live with us and be one of us. Treat all that we have as yours."

Karna replied, "I accept your friendship without hesitation. I have only one small desire, help me attain it—to engage Arjuna in a single combat."

"Go on, with our blessings," said Duryodhana. "We know that you will place your feet on the head of your foe, whoever he may be."

Arjuna felt stirred by this dialogue. "You are an intruder, you have come unasked, unceremoniously, and I will give you just the treatment any impudent intruder deserves."

"This arena is a public one," retorted Karna. "I have as

* Another name for Arjuna.

much right to be here as anyone else. A true kshatriya has no need to waste his time in words, like the feeble ones of other castes who exhaust themselves in futile arguments. If you have learnt to hold a bow and arrow, let that speak and you will get my immediate answer!"

Now the parties were falling into definite groups, the Pandava brothers surrounding Arjuna on one side, Duryodhana on the opposite side, with Drona, Vidura, and the other elders uncertainly in between. When they faced each other thus, Kunthi—who by certain marks now recognized Karna as her son—swooned away at the prospect of the brothers attacking each other. Kunthi was revived with a sprinkling of sandal paste and rose water by Vidura, who knew Karna's antecedents.

Arjuna, being the son of Indra, the Lord of Cloud and Thunder, was protected by that god, who sent down clouds and mist to obscure Arjuna's presence. Karna, being the son of the Sun God, was bathed in bright light and stood exposed, a perfect target for an archer. At this moment, Kripa, a master of the science of war and a guru for Dhritarashtra's children, addressed Karna. "O warrior, please tell us the names of your father and mother and the name of the royal line you come from. After you mention it, this warrior Arjuna will decide whether to fight or not. He is the son of a King, and you realise that sons of kings will not stoop to fight with men of lesser breed."

At this Karna's face fell. He could not satisfy the formalities of lineage. He stood dumb.

Duryodhana interrupted. "At this very moment, I am installing him as the King of Anga, for which I have the authority." He hurriedly summoned the priests to the arena, went through the ceremony of a coronation, and proclaimed Karna the King of Anga, while the gathering watched in wonder. He then addressed Arjuna, "Now here is the King, he has no objection to engaging you in combat, mere Prince that you are. You see the royal umbrella held over him."

But no actual combat ensued. The duel was mostly verbal, as Bhima came forward to question Karna's kingly status. "I noticed, a little while ago, the driver of the chariot coming down to hug and cheer him. He is no eminent charioteer, as one might have on a battlefield, but an ordinary suta who whips horses and drives his master from place to place. This fellow is this instant dubbed King, but he is no more than the son of a driver. Go, go, you fellow, your hand is made to crack a whip, not to lift a sword or a bow."

Duryodhana argued back, "Karna is not only the King of Anga, but can easily be the ruler of the whole world. He will be equal to five of you or more at any time. If anyone resists this claim, let him ascend his chariot and bend his bow, employing both his hands and feet."

There were confused murmurs in the crowd, some approving, some disapproving. At this moment the sun set and since there could be no combat after sunset, the assembly dispersed. Duryodhana, clasping Karna's hand, led him through a path of lamps lit especially for him.

Presently, Drona gathered all his pupils and announced, "The time has come to demand of you my fee for the training and guidance I have given you. I have waited for this occasion all my life."

When they all assured him that they would give him whatever he asked, he just said, "Now you must march on Panchala, seize their King, whose name is Drupada, and bring him prisoner before me. If you succeed in this effort, you will have fulfilled my lifelong ambition."

Without asking for any word of explanation, they assured him, "We will set out this minute."

"Yes, but listen first to this story," explained Drona. "When I was young, I lived with my father, Bharadwaj, who was a great teacher. He trained me so that I could be a teacher in my time, and if you have learnt anything now, it is all what he had taught me originally. My classmate at that time was the son of one Prishta, who came every day to our hermitage to study in my company and then play with me. We were good friends. When Prishta died, my friend succeeded to the throne. He bade me farewell, and assured me not to hesitate if I needed his help at any time. When my son Aswathama was born, my father was no more and I had a difficult time. When the child cried for milk and I could not get it for him, I felt desperate, and I thought of visiting my friend to ask for a cow. His guards at the palace gate stopped me. I then ordered them to go in and announce to the Prince —as I had known him—that his old friend had come to see him. He made me wait at the gate till the evening, and then two guards escorted me, as if I were a prisoner, to his august presence. As he sat there on a high seat, surrounded by his courtiers, I felt like a beggar looking up at him.

" 'Who are you? What do you want?' he asked majestically. I explained who I was and how I had come to visit him as an old friend. 'Friend!' he repeated sneeringly and looked about. His courtiers sniggered politely, stared at me with surprise, and shook their heads. I repeated the word 'friend' again, whereupon the King from his eminence said, 'Oh, ignorant one, don't you realise that there can be no such thing as friendship between persons of unequal status? How can a king be a friend of a man in want, such as you? Obviously, you have come to ask for something. Yes, that you shall have for travelling so far. I see that you are a brahmin in want, but don't ask for friendship. It can never be. Take the gift and be gone.' He turned to a courtier and said something and continued, 'It may be that we were at some stage thrown together through special circumstances, but don't you realise that time changes everything? There can be no such thing as permanent friendship; it is a childish notion. . . . Now you may go, take the presents they will bring you and go away.'

"I stood speechless with rage. I could not bring myself to

mention my child. I could hardly believe that this was the same man I had played with under the trees of our hermitage until his elders came after him in the evening to take him home. I was too angry to say more than, 'I will wait till the same "time" you speak of comes round to give me a chance to speak to you again.' I turned on my heel and left, while they ran after me with all sorts of gifts in a bundle. I threw the bundle at the palace gate and went home. Thereafter, I wandered here and there, and when I came to this city, Bhishma recognized me and engaged me to be your teacher. Now let me demand my fee. Go out all of you, attack Panchala with the best of your arms, chariots, and soldiers, and bring that Drupada back a prisoner, alive. . . ."

Soon the engines of war rolled on, and the young men were delighted to test their skill in arms. In a matter of days, they returned with the booty asked for, King Drupada, as captive. They placed him before their master Drona, who addressed him from his eminent seat: "Aswathama, who is my son, was a child in need of milk when I approached you for help to acquire a cow for his sake. Today, he is a warrior in his own right; he joined my other pupils in besieging your city—all on my order. I could take your life, if I chose, but have no fear. I am not vindictive, still valuing the memory of our boyhood days. I will give you back half your kingdom, unasked. The other half I will keep and rule, so that we may remain equals. I will always be your friend; have no doubt about it."

3 House of Joy—and Ashes

Dhritarashtra, in an excess of affection for his nephews, announced Yudhistira as his heir apparent, and immediately he regretted it. The heir apparent and his brothers appeared to take their roles too earnestly. The brothers together and separately led expeditions around the neighbouring kingdoms, conquered territories, and expanded the empire of Kurus. They became heroes in the eyes of the public, who discussed their exploits constantly.

As became a king, Dhritarashtra constantly enquired of his spies, "What are people talking about?" The spies reported how at the market-place everyone was talking about Arjuna's exploits, the feats of Bhima, or the greatness of Yudhistira. The King would have preferred his sons to be mentioned also, but there was no reference to Duryodhana or his brothers.

He called his chief minister, a man versed in political

subtleties, and asked him confidentially, "Did you notice how Pandu's sons are trying to become popular, overshadowing everyone else? I am not feeling happy about it. You realise that my sons and nephews are equally endowed, but those boys are going too far. Please advise me. You know what I have in mind."

The minister, astute and cunning, replied, "Yes, yes, I understand. I was preparing to bring up this subject myself." He then elaborated on his thesis as to how a king should protect himself from enemies within and without, and how ruthless he should be in guarding himself. "Keep your teeth sharp enough to give a fatal bite at any moment. You should stand in fear even of those from whom you could expect no treachery. Never trust anyone or show your distrust openly. There can be no kith and kin for a king, if Your Majesty will forgive my saying so. We must place our spies not only in foreign kingdoms, but in our midst too; in public gardens, places of amusement, temples, drinking halls; in the homes of ministers, chief priest, chief justice, heir apparent and heir presumptive; and also behind doorkeepers and drivers of chariots. . . . Our sources of information must be widespread and unlimited. Every report, however slight, must be scrutinised and assayed. For a long time I have been considering various measures of security to be enforced in this palace, only now do I dare talk about it." He suggested in a subtle, roundabout manner that the King should exile his nephews.

Duryodhana, after making sure that his father's complacency was shaken, whispered to him in the privacy of his chamber, "We must look to our safety; the time has come. Our spies report that the citizens expect Yudhistira to be crowned any minute. You made a mistake in declaring him heir to the throne. People conclude that you are abdicating because of your handicap, as you had done once in favour of Pandu. We must wake up. I will try to wean away the more important sections among the people with gifts and honours, so that they may start speaking in our favour. It will work, but gradually. Meanwhile, it is important that we get Pandu's sons out of the capital—temporarily, at least. If Pandu's son becomes king, and after him, his son or his brothers, or their sons, and then their sons, we will be nowhere. There is no cause for you to feel alarmed. In your lifetime you will be cared for. Bhishma is here, and Pandu's sons will not dare to touch your person. But others, the sons of the blind ex-King, will be doomed."

Dhritarashtra waited for a chance to speak to Yudhistira, whose hours were fully occupied in the performance of his duties as heir apparent. He consolidated the territories he had won for the King, listened to public grievances, and inspected the army, encouraging the generals with words of praise and decorations. He was accessible to all and sundry, and hardly disturbed his uncle with affairs of the state.

Dhritarashtra waited for two days, and then summoned Yudhistira. "How hard-working you are!" he said. "It is my good fortune to have your help; you have relieved me of much fatiguing work. However, I have begun to feel that you must have a change, some relaxation. I am thinking where you should go if you wish to . . ."

He paused, as if to consider several possibilities. Panic had made him crafty. He had already decided, on the advice of Duryodhana, to send Yudhistira to a place named Varanavata, at a safe distance from the capital. He continued, "During the coming festival of Shiva, the town will be full of gaiety, and I have no doubt you will enjoy this holiday. Take your mother and brothers along; take a lot of gifts with you so that you may distribute presents liberally to artists, performers, and learned men; stay as long as you like at Varanavata. After all, the heir to the throne must become familiar with all parts of the country and must have been seen by all his subjects before he ascends the throne."

Yudhistira understood the implications of this generous offer, but kept his thoughts to himself.

On a certain day fixed by the astrologers, Yudhistira took leave of his uncle and, with his brothers, started for Varanavata in several chariots. A large body of citizens followed, a few among them expressing their suspicion about the motives of the King. Yudhistira assuaged their fears and suspicions. "Our King is our father, concerned with our welfare. He means well for us. We will come back after enjoying our holiday."

As a piece of courtesy, Bhishma and Drona and other elders escorted the Pandavas part of the way, and then turned back. Vidura accompanied them farther, up to the frontier of the capital, where a group of citizens still surrounded them.

Before bidding them farewell, Vidura uttered a warning in a code language: "One who understands his enemy can never be hurt. One should realise that there are sharp weapons, though not of steel, that could strike if one is not watchful. What consumes wood and straw can never reach a hole; remember that the jackal emerges from many outlets underground. The wanderer may know the direction by the stars and survive by firmness of mind."

Yudhistira answered in the same manner, "I have understood."

Later, when the others had left and they were proceeding along, Kunthi remarked, "You and Vidura were conversing in a strange dialect before parting. We could not make out what you were saying. What was it?"

"You will understand in course of time. Let us not talk of it now," replied Yudhistira.

The citizens of Varanavata received the Pandavas with great enthusiasm. They were invited into many homes. They mixed with the crowds and enjoyed the excitement of the Shiva festival. Among those who had received them with a great show of warmth was one Purochana, an architect, who was Duryodhana's agent. He had designed for the Pandavas an exclusive mansion named the House of Joy, fitted with luxurious beds, carpets, and couches of original design, and stocked with food and drink. The five brothers and their mother each had separate accommodations with every comfort.

But when Purochana had left them alone, Yudhistira took Kunthi aside. "The wretch thinks I don't know. Mother, this is what Vidura warned us about. If you sniff deeply, you will notice the smell of oil, resin, and straw, which are packed behind those gilded walls. The man lives here, to ward off suspicion, but he is waiting for a signal from our beloved cousin to start a fire at midnight. Let us be watchful and not betray any sign that we know."

As hoped, a few days later, there came a quiet visitor, a messenger from Vidura. He identified himself by quoting Vidura's parting message to Yudhistira, "Remember the jackal emerges from many outlets . . ." to which Yudhistira replied, "I have understood."

The visitor said, "I am a specialist in digging mines. I can make subterranean tunnels." When Yudhistira took him aside, the miner continued, "Purochana has been ordered to wait for the dark half of the month and start the fire on the fourteenth day at midnight, when you are asleep." With a grim smile, Yudhistira remarked, "How thoughtful of them!"

"I will complete my work well before that time," said the miner. "May I look through this mansion and select a spot for excavation? No one must hear the sound of our crowbars."

In a central portion of the house, a chamber of thick walls and doors, the miner dug up the floor behind closed doors, taking care not to rouse Purochana's suspicion. When the pit was ready, its mouth was covered with planks and camouflaged, while the miner's men went underground and built a tunnel. Purochana, unsuspecting, continued to play the role of steward to the Pandava household, and the citizens of Varanavata never had any inkling of the intrigues and counter-intrigues, but rejoiced to see so much of the Pandava princes in their midst.

When the tunnel was ready, Kunthi invited the public to a grand feast. After the guests had been fed and seen off, Yudhistira said to his brothers, "It is time for us to leave, too."

They opened the secret passage, and after everyone had gotten in, Bhima remained behind to set fire to the house, starting with the room in which Purochana was sleeping. It was a successful conflagration. The material being what it was, very soon the whole building was in flames. By the time the town woke up to it, the Pandavas had proceeded far into the tunnel.

When they emerged at the other end on a river's edge, a boat awaited them with ready sails. The boatman had been engaged by Vidura and established his credentials by repeating the message, "Remember that the jackal emerges from many outlets underground." Then he carried them safely across the river. On the other side, they entered a thick forest, where they wandered aimlessly, wishing only to get far away from Hastinapura.

There was much public mourning and private rejoicing at the news that the Pandavas had perished in a fire. In the mansion named the House of Joy, the charred remains of a woman and her five sons had been discovered. Dhritarashtra had not expected his security measures to be carried so far, and was now conscience stricken. He ordered elaborate obsequies to be performed for the dear departed and country-wide public mourning.

4 Bride for Five

IN THE FOREST, Bhima maintained a watch, while his mother and brothers, overcome with fatigue, slumped down and fell asleep. His heart bled to see them lying on the bare ground. At the thought of their travails, he ground his teeth and swore vengeance on his kinsmen. But through his physical might and courage he was able to mitigate their suffering. He even carried them on his shoulder when one or the other was footsore or tired.

Once he encountered a rakshasa, hiding himself in a mountain cave, who waylaid and ate up any human being passing through the forest. Bhima destroyed him and made the forest safe for others coming after him. The rakshasa's sister, Hidimba, fell in love with Bhima, assumed a beautiful human form, and bore him a son named Ghatotkacha, who always came to his father's aid in any crisis and played a great part in the battle later.

The path ahead seemed endless as the one behind. The exiles had lost all sense of direction or goal. They ate roots and berries or hunted game. They had passed many forests, mountains, and lakes, with nothing clear except that they were going in the right direction, away from Hastinapura. Kunthi asked now and then, "Do you have any idea when and where we shall stop?"

"No," replied Yudhistira, "but I have no doubt that we will have guidance at the right moment." He proceeded along, and the others followed.

One day at dusk, when they were resting beside a lake after the evening ablutions and prayers, they had a venerable visitor. It was their great-grandfather Vyasa, the Island-Born, and composer of *The Mahabharata.* It was a welcome change from the monotony of trudging along in the same company.

Vyasa said, "You see those two paths? Follow the one to your left, and you will arrive at a town called Ekavrata. There you will be quite safe from observation. You will have to behave like brahmins and live quietly and bide your time. Your fortunes will change and circumstances will change. But be patient. Ahead I see victory for your principles. Have no doubt that you will again live in your palace, rule the country, distribute gifts and alms to the needy, and perform grand sacrifices such as the rajasuya and aswametha."

At Ekavrata, Vyasa introduced the Pandavas to a hospitable family who gave them shelter. They were at peace with themselves now, but for the gnawing memory of their cousins' vileness. Yudhistira always calmed them with his philosophy of resignation and hope. Their daily life soon fell into a routine. As became brahmins, they went round the town begging for alms, returned with their collection, and placed it before their mother, who divided it among them. Bhima's needs being greater than those of others, he was given the largest share of food. Thus life went on uneventfully until one day they found their hosts in great grief, arguing among themselves. There was much gloom and lamentation through all their quiet arguments, which were overheard by their guests. There came a stage when the Pandavas could not help asking for an explanation.

Their host said, "On the edge of this town lives a rakshasa who leaves us alone only on condition that every home send up, by turn, a cartload of rice and two buffaloes, to be delivered by a member of the house. He is always so hungry that he consumes the food, the buffaloes, and finally also the person who has brought him the food. We dare not complain, since he threatens to destroy this town if there is any form of resistance. Every home gets its turn; today it is ours. I want to be the one to go and save the younger members of my family, but each one of them wants to be the victim to save the rest. I don't know. I think the best course would be for all of us to be consumed by that demon so that no one will be left to grieve for another. . . ."

After pondering the situation, Kunthi turned to Bhima and said, "You take the food for that rakshasa today."

But when Bhima readily agreed, Yudhistira tried to stop him. "We cannot risk Bhima, nor Arjuna, nor the twins, who are very tender. . . . Let me carry the food for the rakshasa. Even if I perish, Bhima and Arjuna will be able to see you all through your difficult days."

He was overruled by Kunthi. "Let Bhima go; he will come back."

Pushing along a cartload of food and two buffaloes, Bhima arrived on the edge of the town. He drove off the animals before entering the forest, and let out a big shout, calling the demon by his name. "Baka, come out," he called repeatedly, and started eating the food himself. "Hey, you wretch," he dared, "come on and watch me eat. . . ."

The demon came thundering out. "Who are you to call me by name?" He was fierce and immense.

Bhima calmly continued to eat without even turning to look, as the demon came up behind him with all that uproar. Noticing his indifference, the rakshasa hit him from behind, but Bhima went on eating.

"Who are you, eating the food meant for me? Where are the animals?"

Bhima said, "Animals? The buffaloes? They are grazing peacefully somewhere. I drove them off. You will not have them or anything else to eat today. You are on a fast today." He was unconcerned even when the rakshasa belaboured him from behind. "I don't like this disturbance while eating. You must learn to wait."

The rakshasa felt rather bewildered at first, and gave him a few more knocks, but Bhima with his mouth full just flicked him off as if he were a bug on his nape. The rakshasa now tried to pull him away from the heap of food and grab it himself. He could hardly move Bhima from his seat, and when he tried to reach for his food, Bhima warded off his hand indifferently.

"I am hungry, how dare you?" screamed the rakshasa till the forests echoed with his voice. "I will eat you."

"Oh, yes," said Bhima, "I know you will do it, you devil, treating those who bring you food as if they were a side dish. Know that you can't do it any more. . . ."

"Or do you plan to eat me?" asked the rakshasa sneeringly.

"No, I wouldn't relish you, but I can tear you into morsels convenient for jackals and vultures to eat. . . ."

Every attempt that the rakshasa made to seize the heap of rice was frustrated by Bhima, who began to enjoy the game immensely. All the rakshasa's attempts to choke him were equally frustrated. Bhima did not budge until he had polished off every scrap of food he had brought, and then he turned to settle the score with his adversary. A grand fight ensued—they tore up immense trees, hurled boulders and rocks, and hit each other with fists. Finally Bhima lifted the rakshasa over his head, whirled him about, and dashed him on the ground. As he lay limp, Bhima placed his knee over him and broke his back.

The citizens of the town were filled with gratitude and asked in wonder how a brahmin came to possess such strength and valour, qualities which would have been appropriate only in a kshatriya. The Pandavas explained Bhima's talents away by saying that he had mastered certain esoteric mantras which enabled him to overcome even the deadliest adversary.

It soon became necessary for the Pandavas to move on from the hospitable home, where they were now in danger of being recognized. Moreover, a traveller had informed them that Drupada, the King of Panchala, had announced the swayamwara of his daughter, and that he had sent invitations far and wide for prospective bridegrooms to assemble in his palace on a certain day so that the bride might make her choice.

The Story of Drupada

Drupada, smarting under the defeat inflicted on him by the disciples of Drona, had wandered far and wide and found a guru, who instructed him as to how to beget a son who could someday vanquish Drona.

Drupada had performed prayers and sacrifices, and from the sacrificial fire arose a son and a daughter. The son was born bearing arms and encased in armour, and had all the indications of becoming an outstanding warrior. He was named Dhrishtadyumna, meaning "one born with courage, arms, and ornaments." The daughter was dark and beautiful and was called Draupadi and also Panchali.

Draupadi's swayamwara was not an occasion to be missed, so the Pandavas and their mother started for Panchala. There, they occupied an obscure house on the Potters' Street. At the start of each day they went round seeking alms, and brought home their collections to be divided among them by their mother.

On the day of the swayamwara, the Pandavas had left home early and joined the throng moving towards the palace. A vast ground had been cleared and built up with galleries to accommodate the visitors and the young men contending for the Princess's hand. Princelings wearing gaudy decorations and bearing imposing arms had arrived on horseback and chariots.

The day started with elaborate ceremonies performed by the royal priests. At the appointed hour, Draupadi entered the arena and looked around, sending all the young hearts racing. She was escorted by Dhrishtadyumna, her brother, the Prince of the house. He announced that those who would be eligible to be garlanded by the Princess must string a bow kept on a pedestal and shoot five arrows at a revolving target above by looking at its reflection on a pan of oil below.

The princes from the warrior class were the first to approach, but most of them withdrew after one look at the bow. One or two dropped it on their toes. Some could not even stretch the steel coil forming its bowstring.

Draupadi watched the process of elimination with relief. She saw the princes, in imposing battle dress, coming forward haughtily and retreating hastily, galloping away on their horses. Comments, jokes, and laughter filled the air.

The Kauravas were in a group at one corner of the hall contemptuously watching the arrivals and departures. Karna, the most gifted master of arms and archery, was there with Duryodhana. His brothers and henchmen occupied the seats of honour and jeered at the candidates who failed. A lull fell on the assembly when their turn came, and the girl shivered instinctively and prayed to the gods to be saved from them.

She watched with apprehension as Karna approached the bow and lifted it as if it were a toy. He stood it on its end and stretched out the bowstring. But at the very moment when he took aim to shoot the mark, Draupadi was heard to remark, "I will not accept him. . . ." At this, Karna dropped the bow and returned to his seat with a wry smile.

Duryodhana frowned and said in a whisper, "She had no right to talk. If you string the bow and hit the mark, she must accept you. That is the condition. Otherwise, you may seize her and fly off. Go back and take the bow. We will support you."

"No," said Karna, "I don't want her."

In that assembly, unobserved, was a person who was to play a vital role in *The Mahabharata* later. It was Krishna, the King of Dwaraka, actually the eighth incarnation of the god Vishnu, who took his birth in the Yadava clan. He had incarnated as a human being as he had explained:

"For protecting the virtuous
For the destruction of evil, and
For establishing righteousness
I am born from age to age."

He whispered to his brother, Balarama, at his side, "These brahmins are none other than the Pandavas, who were supposed to have perished in a fire. This was all predestined, we will see a great deal of them yet. . . ."

Now there was a stir as Arjuna got up from the brahmin group. There were shouts of protest. "How dare a brahmin enter this contest, which is open only to the warrior class? Let brahmins stick to their scriptures." But King Drupada ruled that he had mentioned no caste in his announcement. Anyone was free to try his luck at the swayamwara.

Draupadi watched anxiously as Arjuna approached the bow. He not only strung the bow, but hit the target again and again, five times. Draupadi approached him with the garland of flowers and slipped it over his neck, and they became betrothed. Arjuna clasped her hand and led her off.

There was a commotion at once. "We have been cheated! How can a brahmin win a kshatriya bride? We will not tolerate it. We will kill King Drupada and carry away the girl." Fighting broke out. Bhima, the strong brother among the Pandavas, armed with the trunks of two huge trees plucked out of the park, guarded the girl while she was taken away to their home in the Potters' Street.

Kunthi was in the kitchen when the brothers arrived. Bhima, wanting to sound lighthearted, cried from the doorstep, "Mother, come out, see what bhiksha we have brought today."

Without coming out, Kunthi answered from the kitchen, "Very well, share it among yourselves."

"Oh!" exclaimed Bhima. "Oh! Oh!" cried everyone, and the loudest exclamation was from Arjuna, who had won the bride.

The mother came out to see why there was such an uproar and cried, "Oh! Who is this? You have won, Arjuna?" She was full of joy, and clasped the girl's hand. "Oh! Arjuna, you have won this bride, this Princess, this lovely creature! So you entered the contest after all. I never believed that you seriously meant to go there. What a risk you took of being discovered by your enemies! How happy I am to welcome this daughter-in-law! Tell me . . . what was the . . . Come in, come in." Her joy was boundless. Her son had won the greatest contest and had come through it safely and gloriously. "Come in, come in. . . ."

They trooped in behind her. She spread out a mat and told the girl to be seated, but, like a well-mannered daughter-in-law, Draupadi would not be seated when the men and mother-in-law were standing. Moreover, her mind was all in a whirl.

There was an awkward pause as the five brothers stood around uncertainly and Draupadi stood apart with downcast eyes, trying not to stare at the five men who were to share her, if the mother's injunction was to be obeyed. What a predicament for the girl, who thought that she was marrying one man and found four others thrown in unexpectedly!

Now Draupadi studied the five brothers as unobtrusively as possible, wondering what freak of fate had brought her to this pass. Kunthi tried to make light of her own advice and said with a simper, "Of course I did not know what you meant when you said you had brought bhiksha. I thought it was the usual gift of alms . . . ." Her voice trailed away.

Bhima the strong, incapable of the subtleties of speech, struggled to explain himself. "I . . . meant to be jocular, I meant . . ."

It was Arjuna who broke the awkward moment. "Mother, your word has always been a command to us, and its authority is inescapable. How can it be otherwise? We will share Draupadi as you have commanded."

"No, no, no . . ." cried the mother.

Yudhistira said, "Arjuna! What preposterous suggestion are you making in jest? A woman married to one man is a wife, to two, three, four, or five, a public woman. She is sinful. Whoever heard of such a thing!"

The mother said, "Don't make too much of an inadvertent bit of advice. You make me feel very unhappy and guilty, my son. Don't even suggest such an outrage."

Arjuna pleaded, "Please don't make me a sinner; it is not fair to condemn me to suffer the sin of disobedience to a mother's word. You, my eldest brother, you are a man with a judicious mind and a knowledge of right and wrong. We four brothers and this girl will be bound by your words. You must advise us as to what is good and fair. Advise us, and we shall be bound by your words, but bear in mind that we cannot go back on the command of a mother. . . ."

When he said this, all the brothers studied the face of the girl, and their hearts beat faster, for already Manmatha, the God of Love, was at work, stirring their blood and affecting their vision.

Yudhistira brooded for only a moment, recollected the

words of a seer who had already prophesied this situation. Deciding to avoid heart-burning amongst the brothers, he declared, "This rare creature shall be wife to all of us."

The King of Panchala, father of Draupadi, summoned the Pandavas to discuss the arrangements for the wedding. The five brothers with their mother and the girl were invited to the palace to be honoured and feasted. They were taken through the palace and its grounds, where fruits, souvenirs, rare art objects, sculpture, paintings, carvings, gold-inlaid leather, furniture of rare designs, agricultural implements, chariots, and horses were displayed. When they passed through the hall where swords, arms, shields, and equipment of warfare were kept, the five brothers picked up the articles, admiring them and commenting among themselves, spending more time in this part of the palace than anywhere else.

Observing this, the King suspected that they might be warriors, although they were disguised as brahmins. When they repaired to the chamber and were settled comfortably, the King said point-blank to Yudhistira, "I know you will always speak the truth. Tell me who you are."

And Yudhistira declared his identity and that of his brothers, and explained their trials and tribulations since the time of their leaving their kingdom a year before.

Now the King said, "Let us rejoice that this day your brother Arjuna, the man with the mighty arm, will marry my daughter, and let us celebrate this union of our families in style. Let us make everyone in this world happy today."

Yudhistira replied, "I am the eldest and still unmarried. I must be the first to marry, according to our law. Please give me your blessings to be married first."

"So be it," said the King, little dreaming of the implication. "You are the eldest, my daughter now belongs to your family. If you decide to marry her yourself, you will be free to do so, or you may give her to whomever you like among your brothers. I have nothing more to say."

"Now," said Yudhistira simply and quietly, "Draupadi will have to be married to all of us." He explained how it had come about and concluded, "We have always shared everything and we will never deviate from the practice."

The King was stunned on hearing this. When he recovered his balance, he cried, "One man can take many wives, but one woman taking several husbands has never been approved anywhere, either in practice or in the scriptures. It is something that can never receive approval from any quarter. A man of purity like you, one learned and well equipped in knowledge—what evil power is influencing you to speak thus?"

Yudhistira tried to calm him. "The right way is subtle and complicated. I know I am not deviating from it. O conqueror of the worlds, have no misgivings, give us your permission."

The King said, "You and your venerable mother and my daughter . . . please talk it over among yourselves and tell me what should be done."

At this moment, the sage Vyasa arrived. When all the formalities of greeting were over, the King asked, "Give us your guidance; can a woman marry five men?"

"Not always," answered Vyasa, "but in this particular instance, it is correct. Now listen . . ." He got up and walked into the King's private chamber. The others followed at a distance and waited outside.

The Lives of Draupadi

"Your daughter," said Vyasa, "was called Nalayani in her last birth. She was one of the five ideal women in our land. She was married to a sage called Moudgalya, a leprous man, repulsive in appearance and habits, and cantankerous. She was, however, completely indifferent to his physical state and displayed the utmost devotion to him as a wife. She obeyed all his erratic commands, accepted his fickle moods, submitted herself to all his tyrannical orders, and ate the scraps from his plate. All this she did without hesitation or mental protest, totally effacing her own ego. They spent many years thus, and one day her husband said, 'O beautiful one, perfect wife on earth, you have indeed passed through the severest trial and come through unscathed. Know you that I am neither old nor diseased nor inconsiderate. I assumed this vicious and disgusting appearance in order to test you. You are indeed the most forbearing partner a man could hope for. Ask me for any boon you may fancy, and I will grant it.'

"Nalayani said, 'I want you to love me as five men, assuming five forms, and always coming back to and merging in one form.' And he granted her the wish. He shed his unpleasant appearance in a moment and stood before her as an attractive, virile man—and he could assume four other forms too. The rest of their life was all romance; they travelled far and wide, visited beautiful romantic spots on earth, and led a life of perfect union, not in one, but several worlds. They lived and loved endlessly.

"She never got tired of it, but he did. He told her one day that his life of abandon was at an end and that he was retiring into loneliness and introspection. At this she wailed, 'I am still insatiate. I have lived a wonderful life with you. I want you to continue it for ever.'

"Moudgalya rejected her plea, warded her off as a drag on his spiritual progress, and departed. Whereupon she came down to earth from the dreamy elysium in which she had dwelt and prepared herself to meditate on Ishwara the Almighty. She meditated with great rigour, and when Ishwara appeared before her, she muttered, 'I want my husband, husband, husband. . . .'

" 'You will soon end this identity and will be reborn as a beauty and marry five husbands,' said the god.

" 'Five husbands! God! Why five? I want only one.'

" 'I cannot help it. I heard you say "husband," and that five times,' said Ishwara. And that proved the last word on the subject, since a god's word is unretractable.

"While it seemed as if the god had spoken in jest, he had his purpose. In the vision of a god there is no joking, everything works according to a scheme. Nalayani was reborn as the daughter of Drupada without being conceived in a womb, but out of a sacrificial fire. Justice and goodness have to be reinstated in this world. The Kauravas are evil incarnate; powerful, clever, and accomplished. For the good of mankind, they must be wiped out, and Draupadi will play a great role in it."

Draupadi was wedded to the brothers. At the ceremony, the first to take her hand was the eldest, Yudhistira; next came the mighty Bhima; after him the actual winner, Arjuna; and lastly the twins, Nakula and Sahadeva, one after the other. The Princess was to live with each brother for one full year as his wife, and then pass on to the next. When she lived with one, the others swore to eradicate her image completely from their minds. A very special kind of detachment and discipline was needed to practise this code. Anyone who violated it, even in thought, exiled himself from the family and had to seek expiation in a strenuous pilgrimage to the holy rivers.

5 Uncle's Gift

In Hastinapura there was much uneasiness, since it was now clear that the Pandavas were still alive. "Then who was it that perished in the fire?" the courtiers speculated.

"Our own man—the fool," said Duryodhana, "and a woman with five children, who had come to dine at the feast, and slept off—drank too much wine, I suppose! I have reports that she'd been seen earlier at the feast. . . . The God of Fire took a woman and her five sons, but not the five we had in mind. . . ." And he and his brothers laughed grimly at the joke.

Dhritarashtra was heard to comment on the swayamwara, "Ah, what a glorious choice for our family! Drupada's daughter is a rare creature. I have heard about her indeed! May they flourish and be happy!"

When he caught him alone, Duryodhana berated him for his enthusiasm. "How can you felicitate our arch-enemy Yudhistira? Have you no interest in your own sons? Have you no concern for your own family?" He glared angrily at his father, who, though eyeless, sensed the fury behind his son's speech. He explained with an artificial laugh, "I did not mean it. I was speaking to Vidura, as you know, and I did not want to reveal to him my real feeling in the matter. We have to be careful with him. I would have been really happy if you had won the bride; that's how I had understood it at first, and felt happy too. But later Vidura explained, and one has to be cautious when referring to those boys in his presence."

"Now we must act," continued Dhritarashtra. "Drupada becomes a father-in-law and ally of the Pandavas. His son Dhrishtadyumna is equal to any of us. Drupada has not forgiven or forgotten the fact that his kingdom was cut up, and that he was humiliated by our guru, Drona. Each day he is getting stronger and stronger and will not rest until he has recovered his whole territory. Our guru made a mistake in leaving him alive. Drupada will never forget that we attacked him."

"The Pandavas too had attacked him!" said Duryodhana.

"But their circumstances have changed, and they are in-laws now, and allies, and have a common enemy in us. Mark my words, they will not spare us."

Duryodhana toyed with the idea of bribing Drupada to isolate the Pandavas or poison them . . . and Dhritarashtra, who was a fond parent, listened to him without contradicting him, although he was sceptical of Duryodhana's wisdom in such matters. Dhritarashtra's dilemma was that he loved his sons, but could not hate his brother's sons sufficiently. He knew he was a party to intrigues and unholy decisions, but he could not act on his judgement where his sons were concerned. He had no mind of his own, and was in a perpetual conflict with his better instincts. Whoever spoke to him got his attention. This became more marked now, when Drona and Vidura and Bhishma gathered around him to discuss the Pandavas.

Bhishma said, "The gods have helped them. At least now you may rectify your error. Send them your blessings and gifts, and welcome the daughter-in-law of the house and bless her. Let them all end their exile and come back. Restore to Yudhistira what is rightfully his. As far as I am concerned, all are my grand-nephews; I knew that you supported your son's plan to get them out of your way. But you will have realised by now, I hope, that it is not so easy to get rid of human beings. The Almighty is all seeing. . . ." Vidura spoke on the same lines.

Drona was even more emphatic. "I know what Arjuna can accomplish. I know Drupada and his growing might. His son is no ordinary warrior. I have seen him. I know him. They are building up an invincible camp. Many others will also be joining them soon. Krishna from Dwaraka was also seen there with them. He will bring in the Yadavas and many others to their side. Krishna by himself will be their chief support soon—you will see it. Krishna is no ordinary mortal, remember. . . . Don't let your past error continue and take you down the path of annihilation."

His forthright talk was not to the Kauravas' taste. Later Karna said, "Don't listen to Drona, though he is our master. What does he know of statecraft? He is concerned only with the art of war and nothing else. Bhishma and Vidura, you know, are the Pandava agents in our midst. The wisest course for us would be to take an army and destroy Drupada, and with him also the Pandavas. No other course is open to us. It is said in all our shastras that quick action and force alone can eliminate a threat. Before Drupada grows even stronger, we must act."

In these conflicting counsels Dhritarashtra was bewildered. After much wavering, he called Vidura and said finally, "You must go to Panchala and convey my greetings to Drupada. Invite Yudhistira and his brothers to return home with their bride, and we will settle the question of their future so that the cousins may live in peace with each other."

Vidura went to Panchala carrying presents to the King and his family. He was received cordially and seated in a place of honour. He formally conveyed the greetings from Dhritarashtra and his sons, and invited the Pandavas to return to Hastinapura. As he listened, Yudhistira looked at his brothers, but they waited for him to decide. Yudhistira's mind was filled with misgivings. How could they again trust their uncle at Hastinapura, whose weakness for his sons was notorious? Vidura was perhaps being used, in his innocence, to lure them back to a deathtrap. He just said, "Now, we are living in the hospitality of our father-in-law. We cannot leave without his sanction. We shall abide by his decision."

At this, Drupada said, "How can I ever say that you should go? You are not merely our guests but our sons-in-law. We consider it a privilege to have you in our midst. But at the same time, your uncle has a claim on you too. . . ."

Vidura added, "My brother Dhritarashtra would have himself come to invite you, but for his physical condition. He, however, counts on your good will to be able to receive and bless the bride and the bridegrooms."

Yudhistira once again looked about for guidance. Only a god, who could take in at a glance the past, present, and future, could guide him at this crucial moment.

Krishna happened to be at the court on a visit. He knew that the destiny of the Pandavas was soon to be in his hands. When they turned to him for advice, he said, "I feel that you should all go to Hastinapura, and I will go with you."

On their arrival at Hastinapura, Dhritarashtra received his nephews with every show of affection. Several days later, he told Yudhistira, "I am dividing this kingdom, and your half will be Khandavaprastha. I would like you to settle down there with your brothers, wife, and mother. Your cousins will rule here; and you may each live happily in your own territory."

The Pandavas set out, led by Krishna, for Khandavaprastha, which proved to be nothing more than a desert—but they were happy to have found a place which was their own. They measured out the land and, after purificatory ceremonies, began to build fort walls, moats, and encampments. With Krishna's blessings, and with the services of the architects he had brought from Dwaraka—since they could no longer trust any builder from Hastinapura—in due course, a brilliant city came into being. It contained a palace with every luxury; mansions; broad roads and highways, shaded with trees; fountains and squares; and shops filled with rare merchandise. Many citizens and traders from Hastinapura came to reside there, attracted by its beauty and convenience. The name of the city was changed to Indraprastha, since it matched the splendour of the City of God.

When they were settled, Yudhistira had a visit from Sage Narada.* Narada wished to see for himself how well the Pandavas had settled at Indraprastha. He spoke at length to Yudhistira on the duties of a king, and then passed on to the problems that were likely to arise among brothers possessing a common wife. He advised that at the time she was possessed by one, the others must not only avoid all thoughts of her, but take care never to intrude into the privacy of the couple. The penalty for such a lapse was also decreed—exile

* Sage Narada moved with ease in the several worlds of gods and men, taking an interest in all their affairs, involving himself and enjoying the involvement. Often he carried information and secrets from one quarter to another, stirring up challenge, controversy, and conflict. Though he enjoyed the agitations and troubles, ultimately, being a seer, he resolved them for their own benefit. Most episodes in the legends, such as Harischandra and Viswamitra, arise from the complications created by Narada's talk.

for twelve years. To illustrate his warnings, Narada narrated the story of Sunda and Upasunda, two invincible brothers, demons who ruled the world and were deeply attached to each other until they abducted Tilottama, a celestial beauty. In due course they fell out and destroyed each other.

In spite of the restrictions laid down by Narada, one day Arjuna had perforce to intrude when Yudhistira was in Draupadi's company, seeking his guidance on an urgent matter of the state. Exiled for twelve years, he spent his time bathing in holy rivers. In the course of his wanderings, Arjuna also married Ulupi, a princess of the serpent world, and then Subadhra, sister of Krishna.

6 City of Splendour

To commemorate their successful rehabilitation, Yudhistira performed a grand rajasuya sacrifice. Thousands were invited to be present in Indraprastha, Krishna being the most distinguished among them all. The guests were overwhelmed with the hospitality and general grandeur of the new Pandava capital with its mansions, parks, and broad roads. The prosperity of the Pandavas was admired by some and envied by others. Among those in whom envy was stirred was Duryodhana, who along with his uncle, Sakuni, had been a special guest and was given a palace and looked after with extreme concern.

After the sacrificial ceremonies were over, all the visitors left, loaded with presents and honours. Duryodhana felt so comfortable that he extended his stay at Indraprastha as long as he could. Finally, one day he took leave of the Pandavas and left with his uncle Sakuni for Hastinapura. While riding back in his chariot, Duryodhana said with a sigh, "See how well the Pandavas live! And how much they have managed to create—out of that desert land to which they were condemned!"

"They have the grace of gods," said Sakuni, "and they have also laboured hard to achieve prosperity. . . ."

Duryodhana received the remark in silence, and then said, "Did you notice how well every one of the thousands spoke of them and what rare gifts were exchanged?"

"Yes, yes, one could not help noticing all that," replied Sakuni.

"We are doomed," said Duryodhana, "while they are coming up with so many as their allies and friends. . . ."

"After all, they have developed only their portion of land. It need not concern you."

"You do not understand," insisted Duryodhana. "I feel tormented, and unless they are degraded in some way, I shall know no peace. My soul burns at the thought of those worthless cousins sitting up and preening themselves!"

Sakuni laughed at this and said, "Why don't you leave them alone? No use challenging them to a war. In addition to their allies, Arjuna is now armed with his great bow, Gandiva, and with the gift of an inexhaustible quiver."

"Yes, I heard about that shameful thing—how he got it!"

"Nothing so shameful; it was a gift of Agni. He is favoured by the gods. . . ."

"How? Go deeper into it."

"To please Agni, he set the Khandava Forest on fire with his astra. He and his ally Krishna, who professes to be an incarnation, rounded up all the poor beasts and birds, sealed off the exits, and drove them back into the forest. Fledglings and birds and cubs and their parents—all alike were roasted and cooked—because the God of Fire needed to consume animal fat for his own well-being. Arjuna was only too ready to provide it and was rewarded with the Gandiva! Whatever you may say of it, Gandiva has made Arjuna invincible. It is an inescapable fact. We cannot fight with them yet. You made attempts to end their lives, and all your plans failed. Now they are strong and prosperous—leave them alone, I say. Don't go near them; they live in their territory and you in yours. I don't see why you should think of them at all."

"You don't understand, you don't realise the agony I suffer. Do you know how they flaunt their prowess and prosperity and laugh at me? Actually laugh! They stand in a row and laugh at me. They let their servants laugh at me."

"Well, we were treated as honoured guests all along—I cannot imagine they would have laughed at you."

"I tell you, they did openly to my face."

"How? When was it?"

"At their new hall of assembly. . . ."

"What a grand, marvellous building, none to equal it anywhere," said Sakuni. "Again, it is a gift from that divine architect Maya, who was saved from the fire of Khandava Forest. . . ."

"Everything for them seems to have come out of that fire!" said Duryodhana. "*We* should have had an assembly hall of that kind, not they. They don't deserve such a grand structure—after all, Hastinapura is more ancient than Indraprastha. How cunningly built, what polish!" He was lost in the vision of that great structure. Soon he recovered his mood of indignation and said, "There was what looked like a pool with lotus blooms on it, all in a passage. While stepping into it, I tucked up my cloak—it was only a polished marble floor, and they laughed at me for this little mistake. A few yards off was another place which looked like that, and I fell into it and drenched my clothes. I had to change, and they seemed to have watched for it. All of them laughed and joked, especially that wild bull, Bhima. Oh!"

"Oh, forget it, it was not really designed to upset you, as you know. . . ."

"And then there was an open door I tried to pass through, which was actually only a wall. And at an open door I hesitated, taking it to be only a wall. I saw a lovely rose I couldn't pluck since it was only a painting. They were spying on me all the time; they stood about and guffawed at my predicament, including Draupadi . . . that awful woman. Someday it will be my turn to laugh at her, be sure of that. . . ."

After much talk on the same lines, Sakuni said, "Give up the idea of challenging them to a war. Some other way must be found to humiliate them. . . ." He thought over it and said, "Challenge them to a game of dice. Well, I'll help you; we will finish them through it. I know Yudhistira's mind. He can never decline an invitation to a game, though he is a worthless player, the weakest player one could imagine!"

The idea appealed to Duryodhana and he said, "You must help me. First speak to the King and persuade him to invite Yudhistira. . . . I cannot talk to the old man about it."

At Indraprastha, Yudhistira had a visit from Sage Vyasa. Vyasa had come ostensibly to bless him after the rajasuya, but before leaving he uttered a prophecy which made Yudhistira uneasy. "I read the signs and portents. The next thirteen years are going to prove difficult for you. Actions and reactions will be difficult to arrest, and will produce grave consequences. At the end of thirteen years, the entire race of kshatriyas will be wiped out, and you will be the instrument of such a destruction."

After Vyasa left, Yudhistira remained gloomy and reflected, "How can we ward off what is destined to happen? I make this vow: for thirteen years, I will not utter a harsh word to anyone, whatever may happen, whether it be a king, brother, or commoner; I shall not utter any word that may create differences among persons. Harsh words and arguments are at the root of every conflict in the world. I shall avoid them; perhaps in this way I can blunt the edge of fate."

When they reached Hastinapura, without wasting a moment, Sakuni spoke to King Dhritarashtra. He reported in detail on the rajasuya, and the distinguished guests, and the grandeur of the whole business. In conclusion he said, "Your son Duryodhana was received and treated well, but I suspect he is not happy. He has lost his colour, a pallor is coming over him, he has no taste for food, he is brooding, there is some deep disturbance in his mind. We must find out the cause of it."

Dhritarashtra was upset. Immediately he sent for his son Duryodhana and questioned him. "I learn that you have grown pale, and some worry is gnawing you inside. Tell me what it is. We will make you happy again."

Duryodhana described in detail the splendour and richness of all that he had seen in the Pandava country, and concluded, "They are our enemies: that you must understand in the first place."

"No, no," said the old man. "I can make no distinction between you and the Pandavas."

"That may be, but I have a different philosophy. They are our enemies. I have read in the scripture that one who does not feel angered at the rise and prosperity of his enemies is like a mud effigy without any feeling. Jealousy is a normal, legitimate emotion. It is our duty to match their luxury and excel them, and impoverish them when the time comes."

Dhritarashtra, though he disputed his son's view, ultimately weakened and agreed to do his bidding. When he heard of the Hall of Marbles at Indraprastha, he decided to build one for Duryodhana immediately. He summoned his minister and ordered, "Let a million men work on this, but I must have this hall of assembly built in the quickest time; it must rise as if by a conjurer's spell. Let the hall be as wide and long as the Lake of Manasarovar, of which I have heard, so that a man standing at one end cannot be seen from the other end. Let there be a thousand marble pillars supporting the roof. Let the roof be set with countless gems and scintillate like a starry night. The Prince has described to me vividly all that he saw at Indraprastha. Gold and the nine kinds of precious stones must be embedded in every wall and pillar—not an inch of space must be left vacant. Let there be no delay. Put up a lotus pond so still that people may want to walk on it. Let the marble on the floor be shining bright so that people might tuck up their garments while stepping over it. Let a million men be engaged."

When the hall was ready, he dispatched Vidura to Indraprastha to invite the Pandavas to visit, as desired by Duryodhana.

Yudhistira felt happy and puzzled when on a certain day Vidura arrived at Indraprastha. After the initial courtesies, Vidura explained, "King Dhritarashtra invites you to visit his new hall, which he has named the Crystal Palace. He is inviting all the princes known to him. He wants you to come without delay, and bring along your brothers, mother, and Panchali. He says that you should stay and enjoy, and also amuse yourself with a game of dice in that distinguished hall." After delivering the message in the official manner, Vidura expressed his personal impressions and judgement. He explained the circumstances under which the hall had come into being. "Nothing that I said could have any effect on him. He is carried away by his son's views and interests, ignoring all else. If you decide not to respond to this call, I can go back and say so. I am, after all, only a messenger."

Yudhistira thought over the invitation, remembering Vyasa's warning. "Could it be pre-ordained?" He had uneasy feelings and said, "Gambling is immoral; it leads to bitterness and conflict. Why should we engage ourselves in such an evil game? We know fully where it will lead us."

Vidura remained silent. He merely repeated, "O King, do what seems to you the best under these circumstances."

Yudhistira said, "When Dhritarashtra commands, how

can I refuse? It is against the kshatriyas' code to refuse when invited to play a game. I will come."

Arriving at Hastinapura, the Pandavas went up to each one of their relations, starting with King Dhritarashtra, and greeted them. Then they were shown their chambers, where they were served food and drink, and were also provided with music to put them to sleep. They were awakened in the morning by bards singing and playing on their instruments. After exercise and repast, having bathed, donned new clothes, prayed, and anointed themselves with sandal paste and perfume, they set out to the assembly hall.

7 Stakes Unmatched

DHRITARASHTRA FELT an inordinate enthusiasm for the coming gambling match between his son and the Pandavas, and was proud of the hall he had built for this purpose. The hall was packed with visitors—rulers from the neighbouring countries and several distinguished guests. In the central portion of the hall, on one side sat Yudhistira, backed by his brothers; on the other, Duryodhana, Sakuni, and their supporters. The royal seats were occupied by Dhritarashtra, with Sanjaya as ever at his side, and Vidura, Karna, Bhishma, and the hundred brothers. When they were all settled and ready to play, Yudhistira said to his opponents, "Please play a fair game and do not try to win by unfair means. Gambling itself is not harmful, but it becomes a vice when deceit is employed."

Sakuni replied, "There can be no such thing as deceit in a game. One who knows how to handle the dice and how to throw them is gifted with a special knowledge and deserves success. He should not be called a cheat. One who knows his dice imparts life to them, and then they obey his commands. How can you call this deceit? There is no such thing. The real evil is the stake; one who stakes irresponsibly and blindly commits a sin. In every contest, whether of arms, wits, or learning, the competent one seeks to defeat the incompetent one; and there is nothing wrong in it. If you have your misgivings, let us not play. We are ready to withdraw."

Yudhistira replied, "Having accepted the challenge, I will not withdraw. Let us begin. With whom am I to play in this assembly? I have wealth, gems, and gold—an inexhaustible source. Whoever can match my stakes, let him begin."

At this point, Duryodhana said, "I am also pouring out my wealth and jewels on this occasion and Sakuni, my uncle, will play on my behalf. . . ."

Yudhistira said, "Playing by proxy is not permissible. But if you insist, let the game begin; here is my stake."

Beginning modestly with a handful of pearls, the stakes grew in size. Yudhistira slipped into a gambler's frenzy, blind to consequences, his vision blurred to all but the ivory-white dice and the chequered board. He forgot who he was, where he was, who else was there, and what was right or wrong. All he knew was the clatter of the rolling dice, followed every few minutes by Sakuni's raucous chant, "I win," and the cheers that burst from Duryodhana's party. Yudhistira was provoked to raise his stakes higher each time Sakuni's voice was heard.

"I have hundreds of women of ethereal beauty and capacity to serve and please. . . . I have a chariot drawn by eight horses before whose pace no mortal can survive; it has gold-inlaid wheels and bells that can ring across the earth. . . ." At each stage he was hoping that the other side would give up, but they accepted the highest challenge calmly as they were in no doubt about Sakuni's "I win." Again and again it happened. The elders in the assembly hall were aghast at the trend of the events. Yudhistira endlessly described the enormous wealth that he possessed in elephants, armies, cattle, and territory, and offered each item in the hope it would be unmatched. But within two minutes, an interval just sufficient to roll the dice, Sakuni would declare, "I win, I win."

Suddenly Sakuni was heard to say to Yudhistira, with a great deal of mock solicitude, "King, I notice that you have lost a great deal. I'll give you time to recollect anything you may still have in your possession, and tell me . . ."

Yudhistira's ego was roused. "Why do you ask for an estimate of my wealth? I have still enough in millions and trillions. You don't have to concern yourself with my limits. . . . Here is . . ."

"I win," declared Sakuni.

"Never mind, I still have cattle, horses, and sheep extending up to the banks of Sindhu. I will play with them, continue."

"I win."

"I have my city, the country, land and wealth, and all dwelling houses . . ."

"I have won."

"Now my wealth consists of my allies, princes. You see them decked in gold and royal ornaments . . ."

"I win."

Within a short time Yudhistira had lost all his dependent princes, soldiers, and attendants, and Sakuni asked with a leer, "Have you anyone left?"

At this point, Vidura said to Dhritarashtra, "This has gone too far. Stop it, and if you are not obeyed, get that jackal in our midst, your son, destroyed. Otherwise, I see the complete destruction of your entire family, sooner or later. To save a family or a clan it is proper to sacrifice an individual. Even at birth, Duryodhana never cried like a baby, but let out a howl like a jackal which everyone understood as an evil sign. They advised you to destroy that monster forthwith, but you have allowed him to flourish in your family. You are partial to him and accept all his demands, and you have sanctioned this monstrous game, which is undermining the Pandava family. But remember that this setback to them is illusory; whatever they lose now, they will recover later with a vengeance. Before it is too late, stop it and order Dhananjaya* to kill Duryodhana here and now, and you will save the entire race. . . ."

It took a lot of courage to offer a suggestion like this openly, but Vidura was sure of his stand, and saw that Sakuni was practising some subtle deceit. "Those who collect honey after ascending giddy heights never notice that they are about to step off the precipice at their back," continued Vidura. "O King, you have enough wealth, you do not have to earn by gambling. . . . The Pandavas themselves won to your side could prove to be your greatest wealth. You will not need anything more. Dismiss Sakuni at once, let him go back to his country. Don't carry on this contest with the Pandavas. . . ."

Duryodhana was annoyed at this advice and said, "Vidura, you have always been a champion of our enemies and have detested the sons of Dhritarashtra, to whom you owe your food and shelter. I only follow my conscience, which tells me to do this or that, and I see nothing wrong in it. You follow your conscience and I will follow mine, even if it takes me down to perdition. If we do not suit your temperament, go away wherever you please."

Vidura turned to the old King. "All right, I will leave now," he stated. "You are fickle minded and partial to this jackal in your family. You think that your sons are your well-wishers, and if you wish to follow them to your doom, I can't prevent you. Any advice I give will be like a medicine rejected by a diseased man, a man who is dying. . . ." But after saying this, he stayed on, not having the heart to aban-

* Another name for Arjuna.

don the old King to his fate. Dhritarashtra remained silent.

Yudhistira looked around and, pointing to his youngest brother, Nakula, who was standing behind him, said, "He is the brother I adore; he is my wealth. . . ."

"I win," declared Sakuni, and beckoned Nakula to walk over to his side. There was hardly any pause before Yudhistira turned to point at Sahadeva next and said, "Sahadeva is the most learned and wise youth, whose knowledge of justice in all the worlds . . ."

"I win," said Sakuni, and Sahadeva was summoned to cross over to the winner's side. Sakuni eyed the remaining two brothers and added slyly, "Bhima and Arjuna, they are your mother's sons, while those two are only your stepmother Madri's sons, whom you could afford to stake away. . . ." Yudhistira's anger rose at this insinuation, and he cried, "How your evil mind works! You are trying to impute partiality to me, and bring a division amongst us. . . ."

Sakuni responded with a great deal of humility, and with a bow, "Forgive me, O King, you know when carried away by his success a gambler is likely to rant whatever comes to his mind, words which one would not dare to speak even in a dream. Forgive my levity. . . ."

Yudhistira pointed at Arjuna and declared, "Here is the one, perhaps the greatest hero, who should not be staked, but I will. Let us see . . ."

"I win," Sakuni said again, and added, "Now, any one left?" Looking at Bhima, he caressed the dice between his fingers.

Yudhistira rose to the occasion. "Yes, I will now stake Bhimasena, wielder of the thunderbolt, who has no equal in strength, a pulveriser of foes . . ."

"I win," said Sakuni and asked, "Is there anything or anyone you have not lost?"

With the dice poised and ready, Yudhistira replied, "I alone am still not won. I will stake myself and do whatever is to be done by one lost to you."

Again came the words, "I win." Sakuni said now, "Only the Princess of Panchala is left; will she not feel lonely with all her husbands gone suddenly in this manner?"

Yudhistira, having lost his judgement completely, replied, "Yes, that sounds reasonable. Panchali is like the goddess Lakshmi, the spouse of Lord Vishnu at Vaikunta," and then he launched into a lengthy description of her. "She is the goddess Lakshmi herself in stature, grace, and complexion; eyes like lotus petals; a woman who is an ideal wife to guide, serve, and sustain a man at all times. Oh! Suvala*, with her our luck will now turn and we will win back every bit we have lost so far. . . . She is our symbol of luck and prosperity, now I will stake her. . . ."

When Yudhistira said this, there was an outcry of protest in the assembly. Vidura hung down his head, unable to bear the spectacle. Dussasana and Karna laughed derisively. Dhritarashtra, alternating between righteous conduct and bias towards his son, could not contain himself, but eagerly asked, "Has she been won, has she been won?" He heard the dice roll and Sakuni say with gusto, "Yes, Maharaja, I have won. . . ."

Duryodhana jumped up and embraced his uncle in sheer joy and cried, "You are . . . you are a master, a great master indeed. None your equal in the seven worlds. . . ." Then he turned to Vidura and commanded, "Go, get that beloved wife of the Pandavas. Let her learn her duties as a sweeper of the chambers of noble men, and how to wait on their pleasure. . . . Go, bring her. . . ."

Vidura was infuriated and replied, "You jackal in human form, don't talk. You are provoking the tigers. When destruction begins, it will be total, caused by you and your indulgent, thoughtless father. Even now it is not too late . . . don't utter such irresponsible, sinful words. . . ."

Duryodhana turned to an attendant. "This Vidura has lost his sense and is raving. He does not like us; he is the jackal

* Another name for Sakuni.

in our midst. You go and tell Panchali that she is no longer a princess but a slave won by us and that we command her to come hither, without a moment's delay. . . ."

The attendant hurried on to Draupadi's chambers and conveyed the message apologetically. In a short while he returned. "She has asked me to bring back an answer to this question, 'Whom did Yudhistira lose first, me or himself? Whose lord were you at the time you lost me?' " He addressed the question to Yudhistira, who looked at the floor, unable to face anyone.

At this moment Duryodhana ordered, "Let her first come, and then put the question to her late lord herself; and the assembly shall hear the words that pass between them." The messenger went to Draupadi and again came back without her. Duryodhana asked him to go out a third time. When this attendant hesitated, he turned to his brother Dussasana and said, "Perhaps this fellow is a coward, afraid of this ruffian, Bhimasena, but he doesn't know he can do nothing now, being our slave. . . . Go and bring her without a moment's delay. She has no right to question and dawdle. She is a puppet for us to handle. Go and bring her here."

When Dussasana appeared, Draupadi said again, "I must have an answer to my question. Did Yudhistira lose me before or after he lost himself?"

"What is that to you?" asked Dussasana.

She replied, "If he had lost himself first, he could have no right to stake me, and so . . ."

"Stop your argument. Will you follow me to the assembly or not?" As he approached her, she shrank back saying, "I cannot come before any one today . . . I am in the woman's month . . . I am clad in a single wrap . . . go away. . . ." She tried to escape him by attempting to run into the women's apartments. Dussasana sprang on her, seized her by the hair, and dragged her along to the assembly hall. . . .

"I am in my monthly period . . . clad in a single piece. . . ."

"Whether in your season or out of it, or clad in one piece

or none, we don't care. We have won you by fair means and you are our slave. . . ."

With her tresses and sari in disarray through Dussasana's rude handling, Draupadi looked piteous as she stood in the centre of that vast assembly facing the elders and guests. "This is monstrous," she cried. "Is morality gone? Or else how can you be looking on this atrocity? There are my husbands—five, not one as for others—and they look paralysed! While I hoped Bhima alone could crush with his thumb the perpetrators of this horrible act, I do not understand why they stand there transfixed, speechless and like imbeciles. . . ."

Karna, Dussasana, and Sakuni laughed at her and uttered jokes and also called her "slave" several times. She looked at their family elder, Bhishma, pleadingly and he said, "O daughter of Drupada, the question of morality is difficult to answer. Yudhistira voluntarily entered the dice game and voluntarily offered the stakes. Sakuni is a subtle player, but Yudhistira went on recklessly. I am unable to decide on the question you have raised. While he played and staked out of his own free will, we can have nothing to say, as long as he was the master, but after he had lost himself, how far could he have the authority to stake his wife? On the other hand, a husband may have the absolute right to dispose of his wife in any manner he pleases, even if he has become a pauper and a slave. . . . I am unable to decide this issue. . . ."

Draupadi was undaunted. "How can you say that he voluntarily entered this evil game? Everyone knew that the King had no skill, but he was inveigled into facing a cunning gambler like Sakuni. How can you say that he played voluntarily, or that the staking was voluntary? He was involved and compelled and lost his sense. He acted like one drugged and dragged. Again, I ask the mighty minds assembled here, when he put up his stake, did anyone notice whether the other side put up a matching stake? Did Duryodhana offer his wife or his brothers? This has all been one-sided. The deceitful player knows he can twist the dice to his own advantage and so does not have to offer a matching stake. Yudhistira in his magnanimity never even noticed this lapse. All wise minds gathered here, saintly men, equal to Brihaspathi in wisdom, you elders and kinsmen of the Kauravas, reflect on my words and judge, answer the points I have raised here . . ." Saying this, she broke down and wept.

Bhima, who had stood silently till now, burst out, "Yudhistira, there have been other gamblers in this world, thousands of them. Even the worst among them never thought of staking a woman, but you have excelled others in this respect. You have staked all the women in our service, and also your wife, without a thought. I did not mind your losing all the precious wealth and gems we had, but what you have done to this innocent creature! Looking at her plight now, O brother, I want to burn those hands of yours. . . . Sahadeva, bring some fire. I shall scorch those hands diseased with gambling. Or give me leave to smash these monsters . . . ."

Arjuna placated Bhima. "When you talk thus, you actually fulfil the aim of our enemies, who would have us discard our eldest brother. Yudhistira responded to the summons to play dice, much against his will."

Bhima answered rather grimly, "Yes, I know it. If I hadn't thought that the King had acted according to kshatriya usage, I would myself have seized his hands and thrust them into fire."

Seeing the distress of the Pandavas and of Draupadi, Vikarna, one of the younger sons of Dhritarashtra, said, "This unfortunate person has asked a question which has not been answered. Bhishma, Drona, Dhritarashtra, and even Vidura turn away and remain silent. Will no one give an answer?" He paused and looked around and repeated Draupadi's question, but no one spoke. Finally he said, "Whether you Kings of the earth answer or not, I will speak out my mind. It has been said that drinking, gambling, hunting, and the enjoyment of women in excess will bring down a king, however well protected and strong he might be. People should not attach any value or authority to acts done by anyone under the intoxication of wine, women, or dice. This rare being, Yudhistira, engaged himself in an unwholesome game, steeped himself in it, staked everything—including Draupadi—at the instigation of the wily Sakuni. She is the common wife of the other four also, and the King had first lost himself and then staked her. Reflecting on these things, I declare that Draupadi has not been won at all." A loud applause resounded through the hall and his supporters cursed Sakuni aloud.

At this point, Karna stood up and motioned everyone to remain quiet. "This Vikarna is an immature youth, not fit to address an august assembly of elders. It is not for him to tell us what is right or wrong, the presumptuous fellow! Yudhistira gambled and staked with his eyes wide open. Don't consider him an innocent simpleton, he knew what he was doing. He knew when he staked Draupadi, he was offering his wife. Whatever has been won has been won justly. Here take off the princely robes on those brothers. Moreover, what woman in any world would take five husbands? What does one call the like of her? I will unhesitatingly call her a whore. To bring her here, whatever her state, is no sin or act that should cause surprise. You, Yudhistira and the rest, take off your princely robes and come aside."

At this order, the Pandavas took off their coats and gowns and threw them down and stood in their loincloths. Duryodhana ordered, "Disrobe her too. . . ."

Dussasana seized Draupadi's sari and began to pull it off. She cried, "My husbands, warrior husbands, elders look on helplessly. Oh God, I can expect no help from any of you. . . ." As Dussasana went on tugging at her dress, she cried, "O God Krishna! Incarnation of Vishnu, Hari, help me." In a state of total surrender to God's will, she let go her sari with her hands raised to cover her face, eyes shut in deep meditation.

The god responded. As one piece of garment was unwound and pulled off, another appeared in its place, and another, and another, endlessly. Dussasana withdrew in fatigue, as a huge mass of cloth unwound from Draupadi's body lay in a heap on one side. But her original sari was still on her.

Everyone was moved by this miracle and cursed Duryodhana. Bhima loudly swore, "If I do not tear open this wretch's chest someday in battle and quaff his blood . . ."

When the novelty of the miracle wore off, the Kauravas engaged themselves again in bantering and baiting their victims. Duryodhana said, "Let the younger Pandava brothers swear here and now that they will not respect Yudhistira's commands any more. Then we will set Panchali free."

Bhimasena cried, "If Yudhistira commands me, I will slay you all with my bare hands. I don't need a sword to deal with rats."

Duryodhana bared his thigh and gestured to Draupadi to come to his lap. This maddened Bhimasena and he swore at that moment, "If I do not smash that thigh into a pulp some day . . ." The Kauravas all laughed.

Karna said, "O beautiful one, those ex-lords have no more right over you; slaves can have no rights. Now go into the inner chambers and begin your servitude as we direct. . . ."

Finally, Vidura said to Dhritarashtra, "Stop all this mean talk, O King. Although they stand here apparently in misery, they have the protection of God."

Dhritarashtra felt repentant, summoned Draupadi, and said, "Daughter, even in this trial you have stood undaunted, holding on to virtue. Please ask for any favour and I will grant it."

Promptly Panchali said, "Please free Yudhistira from slavery."

"Granted," said Dhritarashtra, and since he was in a boon-granting mood, he added, "Ask for another boon."

"Let all his brothers be freed."

"Granted," the king replied. "Now you may ask for a third boon."

"I do not want anything more."

Dhritarashtra turned to his nephew. "Yudhistira, you may take back all that you have lost—wealth, status, and kingdom. Now speed back to Indraprastha and rule in peace. Don't have any ill will for your cousins. Don't forget that you are all of one family. Go away in peace."

Presently the five brothers and Draupadi got into their chariots and started back for Indraprastha.

After they were gone, Duryodhana, Sakuni, and Karna held a consultation among themselves. Karna said, "The brothers have been saved by the woman's intercession—the shameless creature; it is not safe to let them go free like this. We will be attacked as soon as they find the time to sit and brood on all that has happened."

Duryodhana once again got the ear of his old father. "You have undone everything . . . everything. We carefully trapped the cobra and its family, but before the fangs could be pulled out, you have removed the lid of the basket and let them loose. Don't imagine they will be gone; they will come back to finish us."

"What parable is this?" asked the old King, puzzled. Duryodhana explained, "Your nephews, who are such favourites of yours, are on their way to Indraprastha, their glamorous capital. Tomorrow at this time they will reach it. A day after this time they will be starting back with their forces, their allied forces, and all the satellites hanging on their favours, and will come back here in double-quick time and fall on us. We shall have no time to rally our forces or protect ourselves in any manner. Yudhistira's mind is too complex for us to understand. He will have made up his mind to regain his dignity, and you heard what that mound of flesh, Bhimasena, has promised to do to us. . . ."

As he went on, the picture became so terrifying that the old King cried, "What shall we do now?"

"Call them back for another game, and this time they shall finally be dealt with. Get them back before they reach Indraprastha. Once they are on their soil, they may not care for your summons. Let your fastest courier fly to them. This time they shall be dealt with satisfactorily. . . ."

"How?"

"You don't have to bother about all those details. Leave it to us. Uncle Sakuni will manage. Only employ your authority to get them back here in the quickest time."

The King immediately dispatched a messenger to summon Yudhistira and his party back to Hastinapura. Learning of this decision, Gandhari, his wife wailed, "When Duryodhana was born, he howled ominously, like a jackal, and the seer Vidura advised, 'Throw away this child and let him perish; otherwise our entire dynasty will be destroyed when he grows up. . . .' Now I understand what he meant. O King, ignore this son or cast him away and save our race. Don't join in his malicious plans, don't be the cause of the destruction of our race."

Dhritarashtra just said, "If our race is destined to be destroyed, how can I or anyone prevent it? I cannot displease my sons. Let the Pandavas return and resume the game."

The messenger reached Yudhistira when he had gone halfway to Indraprastha. "The King, your royal uncle, wants me to say, 'The assembly is ready again, O Yudhistira, son of Pandu, come and cast the dice.' "

Yudhistira thought it over, and looked at his brothers and wife, who stood speechless, unable to comment. He was always their leader and they could make no decisions. Yudhistira said, "What God wills we cannot avoid. It is the King's summons again. I must go back and play. . . ." Impelled by the gambler's inescapable instinct to try a last chance, he turned his chariot round and drove back to Hastinapura.

The onlookers and the gambling parties took their respective seats in the hall. Sakuni spoke first. "The King has given you back everything you had lost. That is well, we cannot question His Majesty's actions. But now there is going to be a different kind of stake. At the end of this game, the loser will go into exile, barefoot, and dressed in deerskin. He must live in the forests for twelve years, and then in a city incognito for one full year. In that year of hiding, if he is recognized, there must be another term of twelve-year banishment. If you defeat us in this game, we will go into exile immediately for twelve years, and if you are defeated, you will go through it right from the moment you lose."

Yudhistira, as usual, needed no persuasion to say "yes" to the proposal. Sakuni threw the dice and said, "I win."

Not long after, one by one, the Pandavas once again had to cast off their glittering royal robes. They dressed themselves in deerskin and prepared to leave for the forests. Again they were taunted by the victors. Dussasana said to Draupadi, "Your father planned a noble life for you, and now you have ended up with these vagrants. What good will they do you clad in deerskin and begging? This is your time to choose a proper husband out of the nobles assembled here, someone who will not sell you. Those brothers are now like corn without the kernel. . . ."

Bhima nearly jumped on him and said, "You pierce our hearts with these words; I promise I will pierce yours with real arrows, when I remind you of these words someday. . . ."

Dussasana clapped his hands and almost danced around their victims, jeering, "Oh, cows, cows."* As they were moving out, Duryodhana, setting aside all his dignity, walked behind Bhima, mimicking his strides and manner.

Bhima turned round and said, "You gain nothing by this buffoonery; we shall all recall this when I split your thighs with my mace and trample on your head."

* A derogatory term in this context.

Arjuna, Nakula, and Sahadeva also promised to take revenge, each in his own way. They then went up to Dhritarashtra and all the elders of the family and bade them farewell. Vidura suggested, "Let your mother, Kunthi, stay behind in my home. I will look after her till you are all back from your exile."

When he got a chance to talk to Vidura privately, King Dhritarashtra asked, "Tell me how and in what state the Pandavas left." He was, as usual, torn between tender feelings for his nephews and an inability to displease his son Duryodhana. The King was filled with self-blame, anxiety, and a blind hope that everything would turn out all right—as if after a bad dream—and that he would hear someone say that the Pandavas actually did not suffer, but were happy and unscathed all through.

But if any such soothsayer was needed, it certainly could not be Vidura. "Yudhistira crossed the street with his head bowed, his face veiled with a piece of of cloth. Bhima looked neither to his left nor right, but fixedly at his mace in hand. Arjuna looked at no one either, but went spraying handfuls of sand around. Yagnaseni* covered her face with her dishevelled tresses, and passed on in the clothes she had been wearing. Nakula and Sahadeva smeared their faces with mud in order not to be recognized. . . . Dhaumya, their priest, walked holding a spike of dharba grass steadily pointing east, and reciting aloud the Sama Veda. . . ."

"What does it all signify?"

"Yudhistira, being a righteous man, covered his face because he knew his look would burn up any one catching his eye; he wishes to save your sons and their friends from this fate. Bhima looked at his own muscle and the weapon in his hand since he wanted to show that in the fourteenth year he'd be employing them to good purpose. Arjuna wished to

---

* Draupadi.

indicate that his arrows would spread out like a cloud of spray when his time came. Dhaumya indicated that he will have an occasion again to recite the Sama Veda and lead the Pandavas back in a procession on their victorious return."

"Alas, alas!" wailed Dhritarashtra. "Is there no way of undoing all this error? Go, someone, go up and call them back. Tell them that I want them to forget everything and come back. I shall earnestly ask them to return. Let them live in peace; let my sons also live in peace and prosperity with nothing lacking."

8 Wanderings

The Pandavas marched on in silence with a group of devoted followers trailing along, until they reached the banks of the Ganga. There they spent the night under a spreading tree. A few among Yudhistira's followers lit a sacrificial fire and melodiously chanted the Vedas, to while away the time.

Yudhistira appealed to them, "Please go back. The forest is too full of risks—reptiles and beasts of prey. We have brought upon ourselves this fate, why should you share it? My brothers are too dispirited even to pluck fruits or hunt animals to provide you food. So please return to your homes."

Some listened to his advice and left, but others refused to go, assuring him that they would look after themselves without proving burdensome in any manner. Yudhistira was touched by their affection, and was unable to check the tears welling up. His sorrow affected everyone.

At this moment, Saunaka, one of the learned men in the group, consoled him with the philosophy. "Griefs and fears by the thousands afflict all men night and day, but affect only the ignorant. Wise men like you should never be overwhelmed by changes of circumstance, which cause poverty, loss of home, kingdom, or of one's kith and kin." He expounded a philosophy of acceptance and resignation, of getting beyond appearances to the core of reality, where one could understand the ephemeral nature of wealth, youth, beauty, and possessions.

Yudhistira explained, "It is not for myself that I feel the loss of a home. I feel for my brothers and Panchali, whom I have involved in this misery. I am sorry for those who are following me. One should have a roof to afford rest and shade to those who seek one's hospitality, otherwise one ceases to be human."

Understanding his predicament, Daumya, his priest, said, "At the beginning creatures were born hungry. In order to help, the Sun tilted himself half the year northward and the other half southward and absorbed the vapours. The moon converted the vapours into clouds and sent down the rain, and created the plant world, which nourishes life, at the same time providing for the six kinds of taste. It is the Sun's energy that supports life. Hence, Yudhistira, you must seek his grace. All ancient kings have supported their dependents by meditating on the Sun."

Yudhistira purified himself with ablutions, and centered his thoughts on the Sun God. Reciting a hymn in his praise, he uttered his one hundred and eight names, standing in knee-deep water and fasting. In answer to his prayers the Sun God appeared, luminous and blazing, offered him a copper bowl, and said, "Let Panchali hold this vessel from this day, and you will have from it an inexhaustible supply of food, as much as you want for twelve years to come, and in the fourteenth year, you will regain your kingdom."

After crossing over to the other bank of Ganga, they

trudged along for many days and reached a forest known as Dwaitavana, where dwelt many hermits, living a life of contemplation amidst nature. The Pandavas could forget their trials momentarily in such enlightened company. With the copper bowl in Draupadi's hands, Yudhistira could provide the hermits as well as his followers with limitless food.

One afternoon Vidura arrived at their retreat. The moment Yudhistira saw the coming chariot, he said to his brothers, "Does Vidura come again to summon us to play dice? Perhaps Sakuni feels that he should appropriate our weapons too, which he did not touch last time." With great apprehension they welcomed the visitor and enquired of his purpose. He replied, "I have been cast away by our King." And he explained the circumstances that led to it.

After the banishment of the Pandavas, Dhritarashtra was filled with regret and summoned Vidura to prescribe for him a course for attaining peace of mind. He had spent many sleepless nights thinking of his brother's children now treading the hard path in the forests. He wanted a salve for his conscience, some agreeable statement from Vidura that the Pandavas would be quite well, that fate had decreed their exile, and that Dhritarashtra was not personally responsible for anything. But Vidura was as outspoken as ever and repeated that Duryodhana should be cast away if their house was to be saved. This irritated the King, who said, "Vidura, you believe in being disagreeable. You hate me and my children. You are partial to the Pandavas and always wish to do things that are agreeable to them."

"As the sick man detests the medicine given to him, so did the King hate the words of advice I uttered. Just as a youthful damsel would spurn the advances of a man of seventy, so did Dhritarashtra spurn my advice. He said, 'Go away for ever. I shall not need your guidance or advice to rule the world. Go where they will heed your words—anywhere you may choose except here. Now go away immediately.' And here I am."

The Pandavas were happy in Vidura's company. But hardly had they settled down to this pleasant state when another messenger arrived post-haste from Hastinapura. It was Sanjaya. He was again received with every courtesy, but he would hardly be seated for a moment. "I am in a great hurry," he explained. "Our King commands Vidura to return immediately. Yesterday the King fell down in a faint at the assembly hall. He had been grief stricken ever since he had expelled Vidura, and lamented, 'I have lopped off my own limb. How can I live? Will he forgive me? Is he alive?' We revived him and then he ordered, 'Go and seek Vidura wherever he may be, and if he is alive, beg him to return. Tell him how I feel like branding my tongue with hot iron for my utterance. Sanjaya, my life depends upon you, go this instant and find him.' "

Vidura had no choice but to return to Hastinapura. On seeing him, Dhritarashtra, who had lain prostrate, sat up and wept with joy. But this situation did not suit his sons.

Sakuni, Duryodhana, and Karna consulted among themselves. "Our King is fickle minded. Someday he is going to send his own chariot for his nephews and offer them the throne, and that is going to be the end of us. We know where they are now. Let us go with a body of picked men and destroy them. We should not let them nurture their grievance and plan revenge for thirteen years. . . ." And soon they made various preparations to go forth and attack the Pandavas in their forest retreat.

At this moment Sage Vyasa, knowing by intuition what was afoot, arrived and advised them to drop their adventure. Turning to Dhritarashtra he said, "Listen to me; I will tell you what will help you. Don't allow this hostility to continue. Your brother's children are only five, yours are a hundred. . . . You have no cause for envy. Command your sons to go out and make their peace with the Pandavas.

Otherwise, as I read the future, at the end of thirteen years the Pandavas will wipe you out of human memory. Heed my warning."

Frightened by this prophecy, Dhritarashtra said, "Please advise my evil-minded sons."

At this moment another sage named Maitreyi arrived on a visit, and Vyasa said, "Let this sage speak to your sons."

After he was seated and shown all the courtesies, Maitreyi said to Dhritarashtra, "I was on a pilgrimage to the holy places and happened to visit Dwaitavana, where I met Yudhistira, his brothers, and Panchali living out the life of forest nomads. I was pained to see them thus, and though Yudhistira is resigned to it, it strikes me as an undeserved suffering." Then, turning to Duryodhana, the rishi said very softly, "O mighty warrior, listen to me. Put an end to all this strife and bitterness and you will be saving your family from annihilation."

Duryodhana received the advice with a cynical smile, slapping his thigh in response and kicking the ground at his feet to show his indifference, whereupon the sage laid a curse on him. "When the time comes, you will reap the fruits of your insolence and Bhima will rip that thigh of yours, which you slap so heroically now."

Dhritarashtra was aghast and begged, "Please take back your curse."

"That I can't, once uttered. However, if your son makes peace with the Pandavas, my curse will not take effect. Otherwise, it will turn out exactly as I have decreed."

Having come to know that Yudhistira had been condemned to a forest life, several friendly kings visited him to ask if they could help him in any way. Yudhistira just said, "Wait for thirteen years. In the fourteenth year, I will need all your help."

Krishna had also arrived from Dwaraka, and spoke with

Yudhistira. "I had to be away on another mission. Otherwise I would have come to Hastinapura and stopped the game which has brought you to this pass. I would have persuaded the Kauravas to give up their sinful ways—or I would have destroyed them all on the spot."

Draupadi was moved by Krishna's sympathy. "My five husbands, gifted warriors of this world, looked on helplessly while I was dragged about, insulted, and disrobed. . . . Dussasana grabbed me by the hair, and if I put up my hands to protect my head, he tugged away the single wrap around my body. He ignored my plea that this was not the time to touch me. . . . Nowhere in the universe has any woman been so vilely handled, and Karna and Dussasana and the others leered and joked and asked me to take a new husband, as if I were a harlot." She broke down and wept at the memory of the incident. "Five warriors—five warriors were my husbands who could not lift a finger to help me, except Bhima who was held back. You alone came to my rescue . . . you heard my call . . . you are my saviour. Arjuna's Gandiva and someone else's mace or sword—of what avail were they when I was dragged before an assembly of monsters?"

Krishna appeased her. "I promise you—Duryodhana, his brothers, Karna, and the evil genius behind them all, Sakuni—all of them will be punished. Their blood will stain the dust. You will see Yudhistira installed on the throne."

After Krishna left, an argument began between Yudhistira and Draupadi. She had faithfully obeyed Yudhistira's commands, but never accepted his philosophy. "To see you—particularly you, whom I have seen in a silken bed and on a golden throne, waited upon by the rulers of the earth—now in this state, mud spattered, clad in deerskin, sleeping on hard ground—oh, it wrings my heart. To see Bhima, who achieves single-handed every victory, now in this distressing state, does it not stir your anger? Arjuna of a thousand arms—as it seems when he sends the arrows, worshipped by celestials and human beings alike—bound hand and foot, does it not make you indignant? Why does not your anger blaze up and consume your enemies? And me, the daughter of Drupada and sister of Dhrishtadyumna, disgraced and forced to live like this! How is it you are so mild? There is no kshatriya who is incapable of anger, so they say, but your attitude does not prove it. You should never forgive a devil, but destroy him without leaving a trace. On this subject, have you not heard the story of Prahlada and his grandson Bali of ancient times? The grandson enquired, 'Tell me, is blind forgiveness superior to judicious anger?' Prahlada, who knew all the subtleties of conduct, answered, 'Child, aggressiveness is not always good, nor is forgiveness. One who is known to be forgiving always suffers and causes his dependents also to suffer. Servants, strangers, and enemies ill-treat him, steal his goods under his very nose, and even try to take his wife away. The evil-minded will never be affected by compassion. Equally bad is indiscriminate anger and the exercise of force. A man of anger and violence will be hated by everyone, and suffer the consequences of his own recklessness. One should show forgiveness or righteous anger as the situation may demand.' "

Yudhistira listened to her patiently and said, "Anger is at all times destructive, and I will not admit that there could be any occasion for its exercise. O beautiful one, one should forgive every injury. There can be no limit to forgiveness. Forgiveness is God and Truth and it is only through divine compassion that the universe is held together. Anger is the root of every destruction in the world. It is impossible for me to accept your philosophy. Everyone worships peace. Our grandfather, Bhishma, as well as Krishna, Vidura, Kripa, and Sanjaya; all of them strive for peace. They will always urge our uncle to adopt peace. He will surely give us back our kingdom someday. If he fails in that duty, then he is bound to suffer. It is not for us to be angry or act in anger. This is my conviction. Patience."

Draupadi replied, "It seems to me that men can never

survive in this world by merely practising tolerance. Excessive tolerance is responsible for the calamity that has befallen you and your brothers. In prosperity and adversity alike you cling to your ideals, fanatically. You are known for your virtuous outlook in the three worlds. It seems to me that you would sooner abandon me and your brothers than abandon your principles. O tiger among men, you practise your philosophy with a steady mind. You have performed grand sacrifices on a scale undreamt of by anyone in this world. Yet, my lord, impelled by I know not what unseen power, you did not hesitate to lose your wealth, kingdom, and all of us, and in a trice reduced us to the level of mendicants and tramps. When I think of it my head reels and I go mad. We are told that it is all God's will and everything happens according to it. We are like straws wafted about by strong winds, I suppose! The mighty God creates illusions and makes every creature destroy its fellows. The Supreme Lord enjoys it all like a child shaping and squashing its clay doll. Sometimes God's behaviour is bewildering. He sees noble, virtuous persons persecuted beyond endurance, but keeps sinners happy and prosperous. I am sorely confused and bewildered. Beholding you in this state and Duryodhana flourishing, I cannot think too highly of God's wisdom or justice. If God is the real author of these acts, he himself must be defiled with the sin of every creature."

Yudhistira felt shocked at this speech. "You speak with profound fluency, but your language is that of an atheist. I do not trade in virtue as merchandise, to weigh its profit and loss. I do what seems to be right only because it is the only way, and not for results. It is not right to censure God, my beloved. Do not slander God. Learn to know him, understand his purpose, bow down to him. It is only by piety that you can attain immortality."

"It is not my purpose to slander God or religion. I am perhaps raving out of my sorrow; take it in that light if you like. And I will continue my lamentations and ravings, if you please. My lord, every creature should perform its legitimate act; otherwise, the distinction between the animate and inanimate will vanish. Those who believe in destiny and those who drift without such beliefs are alike the worst among men; only those who act and perform what is right for their station in life are worthy of praise. Man should decide on his course of action and accomplish it with the instrument of intelligence. Our present state of misery could be remedied only if you acted. If you have the will and the intelligence and proper application, you can regain your kingdom. Sitting on my father's lap, I used to hear such advice from a seer who often visited him in his days of distress."

Before Draupadi had finished, Bhimasena rose and addressed Yudhistira. "Our enemies have snatched away our kingdom not through fair means, but by deceit. Why should we accept that state? It was your weakness and carelessness that brought on this condition. To please you, we have had to accept this calamity . . . to please you. We have let down our friends and well-wishers and gratified our enemies. My greatest regret in life is that we ever listened to you and accepted your guidance; otherwise Arjuna and I could have dealt with those sons of King Dhritarashtra. It was the greatest folly of my life—the memory of it hurts me perpetually—to have spared those fellows. Why should we live in the forest like wild beasts or mendicants holding up a begging bowl—even if the bowl is the gift of the Sun God? Food taken as alms may suit the brahmin, but a kshatriya must fight and earn his food. You have bound yourself hand and foot with several vows and with the cry of religion; but Dhritarashtra and his sons, my lord, regard us not as men disciplined with vows, but as imbeciles. Give up your apathy and feebleness, and become a sovereign again and rule your subjects as a kshatriya should, instead of wasting your precious days amidst animals and recluses. Leave Arjuna and me to clear the way for you. . . ."

Yudhistira brooded on what he had said. "I cannot reproach you for your words and for the feeling behind them. I agree that it was all my mistake. I confess to something now. I agreed to the gambling only with a secret hope that I would be able to snatch away the whole kingdom and sovereignty from Duryodhana and make him my vassal, while we had only half the kingdom after our return from Panchala Desa; but he played with the aid of that expert, Sakuni, and now I am paying for my own cupidity, which I had not confessed to any one till now. Don't decide in anger or hurry; we will not achieve anything through such resolutions. Oh, Bhima, I am pained by your words, please wait patiently for better times. I have given my word that we would remain in exile for thirteen years, and I cannot easily retract it now. Nothing else matters. . . ."

Bhima made a gesture of despair. "We are like froth on the river, drifting with its current, whatever one may think or do. Every moment we are growing older. Thirteen years . . . ! Who knows whether we will be alive or fit to take back our kingdom? And we will have thirteen years less for our existence. We should attempt to wrest back our kingdom this very minute. We have already spent thirteen months in exile. Each month has been like a year, and that is sufficient fulfilment of your promise. You have agreed to remain incognito for a year after the twelve-year exile. How can this condition ever be fulfilled? Dhritarashtra's sons will find out our whereabouts through their spies, and then we will have to go into exile for another twelve years. Is that it? That was an unfair condition for the thirteenth year. How could you agree to it? How could the six of us ever remain unnoticed? Myself particularly, how can I be concealed? You might as well try to hide Mount Meru. . . . O King, now let us plan seriously. . . ."

Yudhistira remained silent for a long time, and then said, "Apart from my promise and the bond thereon, it will not be practical for us to plunge into a conflict now. On his side,

Duryodhana has the support of Bhishma, Drona, and his son Aswathama. All the others, who speak favourably for us now, will join him should a conflict arise, since they are kept and sheltered by him. Furthermore, all the armies of the kings we have punished in our early campaigns will look for an opportunity to muster themselves for an attack against us. We must gather strength and support gradually until we can match our army with theirs. You and Arjuna are on our side, but Drona, his son Aswathama, and Karna, practically invincible men, are on their side. How are we to vanquish all those men? We have no chance of surviving a fight yet. I feel uneasy thinking of all this. I do not know what to do really. . . ."

At this moment Vyasa arrived, and said, "Yudhistira, I read what passes in your mind, and am here to dispel your fears. There will come a time, be assured of it, when Arjuna will slay all your foes in battle. I will impart to you a mantra called Pratismriti, and that will help you. You will impart it to Arjuna, and let him go forth to meet the gods in their worlds and receive from each of them a special weapon. After he obtains them he will become invincible. Don't despair." He took Yudhistira aside and asked him to go through a purificatory bath, and whispered the mantra in his ear. After that, Vyasa departed, tendering a parting advice. "You have stayed in Dwaitavana long enough. Now move on to another suitable place, and you will feel happier there. It is not pleasant to stay in any one place too long."

Presently Yudhistira moved from Dwaitavana with his brothers and Draupadi to reside in Kamyakavana, which offered them a background of lovely lakes and woods. In due course, Yudhistira felt the time ripe to impart the secret mantra to Arjuna. On an auspicious day, after due preparations, he transferred the great mantra to Arjuna and gave him leave to acquire more weapons from Indra, Varuna,

Iswara, and other gods. Arjuna moved northward and soon reached the Vindhya Mountains, where he selected a spot and settled down to meditate.

Shiva appeared to Arjuna, first in the guise of a hunter and then in his true form, granted to him an astra called Pasupatha, and then vanished. Following him, Varuna, Yama, and Kubera came one after another and imparted the techniques of their different special weapons, assuring him success against the Kauravas.

Then on a mountain path he found a chariot waiting to carry him to Indra's city, Amaravathi. Being the son of Indra, he was received with all honours and entertained with music and dance by celestial beings. In due course Indra imparted to him the secrets of his weapons, and then suggested, "You will now learn music and dance, which you will find useful some day." So a gandharva named Chitrasena tutored him in the arts.

During this period, the celestial courtesan Urvasi fell in love with Arjuna and, with Indra's sanction, set out to meet him at night dressed in transparent silk, anointed with perfumes. When she knocked on the door of Arjuna's abode, he received her with profound courtesy, declaring, "You are like my mother Kunthi or Madri. . . ." at which Urvasi felt spurned and asked if he had no manliness left. He told her, "I am under an ascetic vow at this time in order to achieve certain aims and I cannot view you except as my mother." She cursed him, "Since you have disregarded a woman who has been commanded by her lord and your father to please you, may you pass among women unnoticed and treated as a eunuch." She flounced out in a rage. Later, Indra told him, "You have surpassed even the most austere rishis in exercising self-control. Urvasi's curse will bear fruit in the thirteenth year of your exile, when you will find it actually to be a blessing."

At Kamyakavana, missing his company, Arjuna's brothers and wife felt depressed and restless. On the advice of Sage Narada, Yudhistira decided to go on a pilgrimage; to bathe in holy rivers and lakes and pray in all the sacred spots. The Pandavas began their pilgrimage westward, visiting Naimisha Forest on the banks of the Godavari, and then proceeded to the confluence of the Ganga and Yamuna, where the gods were said to come down to perform tapas. They zig-zagged their way through the country, never missing a single mountain or river that had any sacred association. They could now forget their sorrows, although always feeling a perpetual emptiness in their hearts owing to Arjuna's absence. At the end of the twelfth year of exile, they had arrived at a certain spot in the Himalayas, where Arjuna rejoined them after an absence of five years. When he described to them the weapons he had acquired from the divine sources, their hopes rose again, and they began to discuss seriously how to win back their kingdom after the lapse of one more year of exile in disguise. At the end of the pilgrimage they returned to Kamyakavana.

9 Hundred Questions

MEANWHILE, news reached Dhritarashtra through his spies of the movements and achievements of the Pandavas, particularly of Arjuna's additions to his arsenal. Dhritarashtra was, as usual, torn between avuncular sentiments and a desire to preserve himself and his sons. He went off into speculations on what to do, and as usual fell into total confusion. Duryodhana watched his father's reactions with uneasiness and said, "The King cannot forget his nephews; he is obsessed with thoughts of them. Now that we know where they are, why should we not act swiftly and end this nuisance once and for all?"

"That may not prove so easy," said Sakuni. "Arjuna has acquired extraordinary powers and, fired by a sense of revenge, the Pandavas may prove formidable. However, they have still over a year to remain in exile. Yudhistira will not go back on his word, even if the King grows soft and invites them to return home. But you may do one thing. They are now in Kamyaka looking like wandering tribes, clad in animal hide and rolling in dust. Why don't you go up and exhibit yourself in your fullest royal splendour? You are the lord of the world today, enjoying unlimited wealth, power, and authority. It is said that there could be nothing more gratifying than showing off one's superiority before an enemy reduced to beggary. Why don't you establish a royal camp in the vicinity of the Kamyaka Forest, and we will see that they come up before you in their rags to be admitted grudgingly by the gatekeepers?"

On the excuse of having to inspect the cattle grazing on their frontiers, Duryodhana got Dhritarashtra's permission to establish a camp in the vicinity of Kamyaka. The camp was a regal one with hundreds of courtesans, attendants, soldiers, and courtiers. Feasts, dances, music, and entertainment of every kind went on noisily night and day. The whole area was transformed with colourful illuminations and fireworks.

Duryodhana and his accomplices had arrived at the camp in splendid armour and military equipment, in dazzling style. They hoped that the Pandavas would notice the brilliance and gaiety of the camp across the river from Kamyaka. Duryodhana tried to send a messenger to summon the Pandavas before him, but the messenger was denied passage across the river by a watchman, a gandharva sent down by the gods to create a crisis. After heated arguments and protests, a scuffle ensued. Others gradually got involved in the affair.

Starting thus, imperceptibly, a full-fledged fight developed between the armies of the gandharvas and Duryodhana. At the end of the skirmish, after his soldiers had been killed, Duryodhana was taken prisoner with his allies and bound in chains.

Learning of this incident, and of Karna's flight from it, Yudhistira dispatched Bhima and Arjuna to rescue Duryodhana: "After all, they are our brothers, and whatever might be the conflict between us, we cannot abandon them now."

Bhima and Arjuna went into action, and were able to free the prisoners from the gandharvas, who had been instructed by Indra himself to undertake this expedition and teach Duryodhana a lesson. Duryodhana thanked the Pandavas for their help, wound up his camp, and went back to Hastinapura, sadder and wiser. The Pandavas returned to Dwaitavana.

The Pandavas were in a hopeful mood when they came back to their original starting point, Dwaitavana, after their prolonged pilgrimage. Dwaitavana was rich in fruits and roots, and the Pandavas lived on sparse diets, performing austerities and practising rigid vows.

They managed to live, on the whole, a tranquil life—until one day a brahmin arrived in a state of great agitation. He had lost a churning staff and two faggots of a special kind, with which he produced the fire needed for his religious activities. All his hours were normally spent in the performance of rites. But that day, he wailed, "A deer of extraordinary size, with its antlers spreading out like the branches of a tree, dashed in unexpectedly, lowered its head, and stuck the staff and the faggots in its horns, turned round, and vanished before I could understand what was happening. I want your help to recover those articles of prayer, for without them I will not be able to perform my daily rites. You can see its hoof marks on the ground and follow them."

As a kshatriya, Yudhistira felt it his duty to help the brahmin, so with his brothers, he set out to chase the deer. They followed its hoof marks and eventually spotted it, after a long chase. But when they shot their arrows, the deer sprang away, tempted them to follow it here and there, and suddenly vanished without a trace. They were by this time drawn far into the forest and, feeling fatigued and thirsty, they sat under a tree to rest.

Yudhistira told his youngest brother, Nakula, "Climb this tree and look for any sign of water nearby."

Presently, Nakula cried from the top of the tree, "I see some green patches and also hear the cries of cranes . . . must be a water source." He came down and proceeded towards a crystal-clear pond, sapphire-like, reflecting the sky. He fell down on his knees and splashed the water on his face. As he did this, a loud voice, which seemed to come from a crane standing in the water, cried, "Stop! This pond is mine. Don't touch it until you answer my questions. After answering, drink or take away as much water as you like." Nakula's thirst was so searing that he could not wait. He bent down and, cupping his palms, raised the water to his lips. He immediately collapsed, and lay, to all purposes, dead.

After a while, Yudhistira sent his brother, Sahadeva, to see what was delaying Nakula's return. He too rushed forward eagerly at the sight of the blue pond, heard the warning, tasted the water, and fell dead.

Arjuna followed. On hearing the voice, he lifted his bow, shot an arrow in the direction of the voice, and approached the water's edge. The voice said, "Don't be foolhardy. Answer me first before you touch the water."

Arjuna, surveying with shock and sadness the bodies of his younger brothers, replied, "When you are silenced with my arrows, you will cease to question. . . ." Driven to desperation with thirst and enraged at the spectacle of his dead brothers, he sent a rain of arrows in all directions. As the voice continued to warn, "Don't touch," he stooped and took the water to his lips and fell dead.

Next came Bhima. He saw his brothers lying dead, and swung his mace and cried back when he heard the voice, "O evil power, whoever you may be, I will put an end to you presently, but let me first get rid of this deadly thirst. . . ." Turning a deaf ear to the warning, he took the water in the cup of his palm and with the first sip fell dead, the mace rolling away at his side.

Yudhistira himself presently arrived, passing through the forest where no human being had set foot before except his brothers. He was struck by the beauty of the surroundings—enormous woods, resonant with the cry of birds, the occasional grunt of a bear, or the light tread of a deer on dry leaves—and then he came upon the magnificent lake, looking as if made by heavenly hands. There on its bank he saw his brothers.

He wept and lamented aloud. Both the poignancy and the mystery of it tormented him. He saw Arjuna's bow and Bhima's mace lying on the ground, and reflected, "Where is your promise to split Duryodhana's thigh? What was the meaning of the gods' statement at Arjuna's birth that no one could vanquish him?" How was he to explain this calamity to Kunthi?

A little later he said to himself, "This is no ordinary death. I see no marks of injury on any of them. What is behind it all?" Could it be that Duryodhana had pursued them, and had his agents at work? He observed the dead faces; they bore no discolouration or sign of decay. He realised that his brothers could not have been killed by mortals, and concluded that there must be some higher power responsible. Resolving not to act hastily, he considered all the possibilities, and stepped into the lake to perform the rites for the dead.

The voice now said, "Don't act rashly; answer my questions first and then drink and take away as much water as you like. If you disregard me, you will be the fifth corpse here. I am responsible for the deaths of all these brothers of yours; this lake is mine and whoever ignores my voice will die. Take care!"

Yudhistira said humbly, "What god are you to have vanquished these invincible brothers of mine, gifted and endowed with inordinate strength and courage? Your feat is great and I bow to you in homage, but please explain who you are and why you have slain these innocent slakers of thirst? I do not understand your purpose, my mind is agitated and curious. Please tell me who you are."

At this request he saw an immense figure materialising beside the lake, towering over the surroundings. "I am a yaksha. These brothers of yours, though warned, tried to force their way in and have paid for it with their lives. If you wish to live, don't drink this water before you answer my questions."

Yudhistira answered humbly, "O yaksha, I will not covet what is yours. I will not touch this water without your sanction, in spite of my thirst. I will answer your questions as well as I can."

The yaksha asked, "What makes the sun rise? . . . What causes him to set?"

Yudhistira answered, "The Creator Brahma makes the sun rise, and his dharma causes the sun to set. . . ."

Yudhistira had to stand a gruelling test. He had no time even to consider what to say, as the questions came in a continuous stream. Yudhistira was afraid to delay an answer or plead ignorance. Some of the questions sounded fatuous, some of them profound, some obscure but packed with layers of significance. Yudhistira was constantly afraid that he might upset the yaksha and provoke him to commit further damage, although one part of his mind reflected, "What worse fate can befall us?"

Without giving him time to think, the questions came, sometimes four at a time in one breath. Their range was unlimited, and they jumped from one topic to another.

"What is important for those who sow? What is important for those who seek prosperity?" Before Yudhistira could complete his sentence with "Rain," he also had to be answering the next question with "Offspring. . . ."

The yaksha went on to ask, "What is weightier than the earth?"

"Mother."

"Higher than the heavens?"

"Father."

"Faster than the wind?"

"Mind."

"What sleeps with eyes open?"

"Fish."

"What remains immobile after being born?"

"Egg."

"Who is the friend of the exile?"

"The companion on the way."

"Who is the friend of one about to die?"

"The charity done in one's lifetime."

"Who is that friend you could count as God given?"

"A wife."

"What is one's highest duty?"

"To refrain from injury."

To another series of questions on renunciation, Yudhistira gave the answers: "Pride, if renounced, makes one agreeable; anger, if renounced, brings no regret; desire, if renounced, will make one rich; avarice, if renounced, brings one happiness. True tranquility is of the heart. . . . Mercy may be defined as wishing happiness to all creatures. . . . Ignorance is not knowing one's duties. . . . Wickedness consists in speaking ill of others."

"Who is a true brahmin? By birth or study or conduct?"

"Not by birth, but by knowledge of the scriptures and right conduct. A brahmin born to the caste, even if he has mastered the Vedas, must be viewed as of the lowest caste if his heart is impure."

There were a hundred or more questions in all. Yudhistira felt faint from thirst, grief, and suspense, and could only whisper his replies. Finally, the yaksha said, "Answer four more questions, and you may find your brothers—at least one of them—revived. . . . Who is really happy?"

"One who has scanty means but is free from debt; he is truly a happy man."

"What is the greatest wonder?"

"Day after day and hour after hour, people die and corpses are carried along, yet the onlookers never realise that they are also to die one day, but think they will live for ever. This is the greatest wonder of the world."

"What is the Path?"

"The Path is what the great ones have trod. When one looks for it, one will not find it by study of scriptures or arguments, which are contradictory and conflicting."

At the end of these answers, the yaksha said, "From among these brothers of yours, you may choose one to revive."

Yudhistira said, "If I have only a single choice, let my young brother, Nakula, rise."

The yaksha said, "He is after all your stepbrother. I'd have thought you'd want Arjuna or Bhima, who must be dear to you."

"Yes, they are," replied Yudhistira. "But I have had two mothers. If only two in our family are to survive, let both the mothers have one of their sons alive. Let Nakula also live, in fairness to the memory of my other mother Madri."

The yaksha said, "You have indeed pleased me with your humility and the judiciousness of your answers. Now let all your brothers rise up and join you."

The yaksha thereafter revived all his brothers and also conferred on Yudhistira the following boon: "Wherever you may go henceforth, with your brothers and wife, you will have the blessing of being unrecognized." The yaksha was none other than Yama, the God of Justice, and father of Yudhistira, who had come to test Yudhistira's strength of mind and also to bless him with the power to remain incognito—a special boon in view of the conditions laid down for the last year of exile.

The Pandavas' final trial seemed to be over. They had recovered and restored to the brahmin ascetic his churning staff and the burning sticks. Now they could sit calmly in front of their hermitage and talk of their future.

Yudhistira said, "Our twelve years' trial is over. We have one more year to spend. Let us pass it in a city—we have lived in the forests long enough. Arjuna, you have travelled much; suggest where we could spend the coming year."

Arjuna rose to the occasion. "We have the grace of Dharma, your father, and shall not be recognized wherever we may be. All around, there are a number of kingdoms abounding in wealth, comfort, and food. I could mention many prosperous countries—Panchala, Chedi, Matsya, Salva, Avanthi. You could choose any of these for our remaining year's residence. Any one of them will be agreeable and we will not be recognized."

They thought it over. "No, not Panchala, our father-in-law's place, that would be impossible. We must select a place where we may live without fear. The country should also be pleasant and agreeable."

"Of all those you mention," said Yudhistira, "I feel Matsya will be the most suitable one. Its ruler, King Virata, is a good, generous man. Let us spend the year there. Let us seek work in his palace. How shall we enter his service? We have to decide that. As for me, I shall call myself Kanka and offer to keep the King engaged and amused—playing dice with King Virata . . ."

"Dice!" his brothers exclaimed in unison. "Oh!"

"No harm in it," Yudhistira said. "We'll play without stakes, just to while away the time." For a while he was lost in visions of the game. "How pleasant to roll the dice and the tinted pawns of ivory in one's palm. . . ." He roused himself from the colourful vision and continued, "I have no doubt that Virata will find my company most engaging. If he questions me at any time, I'll have to tell him that I used to keep Yudhistira constant company—it would not be a falsehood anyway! What would you choose to do?" he asked Bhima.

Bhima reflected for a moment and said, "I'll name myself Vallabha and offer to work in the King's kitchen." He indulged in a loud dream of how he would enjoy this role. "The King will not have tasted such delicacies in his life. Oh, what a chance to try out my ideas!" He revelled in a vision of feasting and feeding the royal household with divine food and added, "I will also show them some physical feats as a side entertainment, controlling their elephants and bulls, which may prove truculent. I will wrestle with their champions and put them to shame, taking care not to kill anyone. If I am asked to explain my past I will tell them that I was a cook in the employment of Yudhistira and also amused my master with wrestling feats. That wouldn't be a lie, would it?" he asked Yudhistira with a sly smile.

Yudhistira turned to Arjuna and asked, "And how will you take it?"

Arjuna said, "It is going to be difficult to hide the deep marks of the bowstring on my arm, which may betray me. I will have to cover them with a stack of conch bangles up to my elbow. I shall wear a long braid and brilliant ear drops, dress like a woman, and call myself Brihannala, and pass myself off as a neuter. I will seek employment in the ladies' chambers, to guard them, teach them dance and music, and to tell them stories."

"This would be the most complete falsehood!" sighed Yudhistira. "Well, you have no other course, I suppose . . ."

Arjuna explained, "I was cursed in Indra's world by Urvasi to be called a eunuch, and that curse has to be fulfilled. We can't help these things."

"I will call myself Granthika," Nakula declared. "I will take care of the King's stables. I love horses, and understand them. At my touch, the most vicious animal will turn docile and take on a rider or draw a chariot. I can make them fly like a storm. I will say that Yudhistira had engaged me as his stable steward. . . ."

Sahadeva said, "I will offer to look after the King's cattle.

I know all the auspicious marks on a bull, and the moods of the milch cow. At my touch, milk will flow from an udder. I love cattle, and am prepared to spend the rest of my life in their midst."

The brothers looked happy for the first time in twelve years, especially at the prospect of indulging in their favourite hobbies. Yudhistira then thought of Draupadi. "You are delicate, and unused to drudgery," he told her. "You should do no harder job than choosing your perfume or jewellery for the day."

"Don't forget that I have not seen a mirror for twelve years," answered Draupadi, catching their light mood of jocularity. "There is a class of women called Sairandhari who serve as companions or handmaids, mostly in royal households. I shall be the Sairandhari, one skilled in grooming and dressing hair, in Virata's women's chambers. If questioned, I shall state that I served as Draupadi's companion, and that would be as near the truth as need be."

After this they consulted Daumya, their priest. He said, "I don't doubt that you will be happy in the Virata kingdom, but still I warn you. You must take special care of Draupadi. Do not expose her too much to the public gaze. Virata himself is a noble person, but there are one or two in his court who may not be as good. Take special care of her. And another point. In the proximity of a king, you will have to keep in mind a few important rules. Being a king yourself, you will not have known them. Only a commoner serving a king could realise that it is a knife-edge existence. Far happier are those who never see their king except when he passes along, riding an elephant, in a procession. One who serves a king is serving an embodiment of God and must adjust his distance suitably. Never enter the King's presence without announcing yourself and seeking his permission. Never occupy a seat at the court which may rouse the envy of another. Don't offer any counsel unasked. Don't talk unnecessarily or carry any gossip, but remain silent and alert at all times. Never give any occasion for him to repeat a command. In the King's presence one should be gentle in speech and avoid vehemence and the expression of anger or contempt. One should not laugh too loudly nor display undue gravity. One should not dress like the King, nor gesticulate while speaking, nor mention outside what has transpired in the King's presence. Be available to the call of the King but don't be obtrusive." Thus Daumya went on expounding the code to be followed by a courtier. Then he bade them farewell and left to reside in Panchala.

Leaving the forests once and for all, the Pandavas reached the Virata country. Outside the capital, they bundled up their armour, mailcoats, bows, arrows, and swords in a sack and tied it to the top branch of a banyan tree standing in a burial ground. With their hands bare of weapons, they reached the palace gate and announced that they had come to serve the King, who summoned them one by one and engaged them. They remained unrecognized through the grace of Yama.

For almost a year there were no untoward incidents, and they pleased Virata by their diligence and integrity. Only a few days remained to complete their term of exile when a last-minute complication arose unexpectedly.

As feared by Daumya, Draupadi came to be noticed by Kichaka, the Queen's brother and the general of the army, a handsome, powerful man. He had suddenly spied Draupadi while she was serving the Queen, and pursued her with determination as she went about her duties in the palace. Although her husbands noticed her plight, they could not help her without betraying their identity. They comforted her in secret and promised to protect her at the right time. Not only Daumya, but even the Queen had anticipated this situation. "Men, being what they are, will not leave you alone," she had said. "Your beauty frightens me. I fear even my husband, Virata may succumb to your looks. How can I have you in the palace, and avoid complications?"

Draupadi had answered quickly, "Have no fear; there will be no complications. I am married to five gandharvas who are ever watchful though unseen, wherever I may be. They will protect me, and if anyone molests me the gandharvas will kill him immediately. . . ." This had somehow satisfied the Queen, who loved Draupadi's company. She warned her brother not to go near Draupadi, but he ignored her in the fever of his infatuation.

Kichaka asked her to send Draupadi to him on some errand, and when she arrived, tried to take her in his arms. When she repelled him, he was angry and assaulted her. She went tearfully to the King and complained while he was playing dice with Yudhistira. Neither the King nor Yudhistira paid any attention to her, though the latter felt shocked, and checked himself.

She then sought Bhima's help, bitterly complaining against others, particularly Yudhistira, who would not interrupt his play. Bhima promised her his help, and they evolved a plan. She was to lure Kichaka to visit a dance hall late at night, promising to yield to him there. Kichaka fell into this trap, and when he stepped into the darkened hall, he was hugged by Bhima, and disposed of quickly.

Kichaka's death created a sensation in the country since he had been a powerful man and the head of the army. Draupadi explained that he had been destroyed by her gandharva husbands. There was public mourning, and the citizens looked on Draupadi as an evil spirit in their midst, seized her, and prepared to cremate her on Kichaka's funeral pyre. Bhima rescued her at the last minute, secretly destroying, in the operation, Kichaka's soldiers, who were carrying her off to the pyre. When she went back to the palace, both the King and Queen became nervous. The Queen pleaded, "Sairandhari, please go away. We dare not keep you with us. The fate that overtook my brother and hundreds of his followers may overtake us too. We are afraid of your gandharva protectors, not knowing when they will be roused. I like you but I cannot have you here. Please leave us. Go far away."

Draupadi said, "Please don't be harsh. Your brother provoked my husbands—otherwise, no harm would have come to him. I assure you they will not harm you, since you have all been so kind to me. Please let me stay for only thirteen days more. I have some special reason for making this request, and I will go away after thirteen days, I promise. Please show me this consideration."

The Queen thought it over, looked at Draupadi searchingly, and asked, "Why thirteen days?"

"I can't explain now, but you will know . . ."

"Will you keep off your gandharvas?

"I promise on my honour. They will never come near this palace again."

"You may stay on. I shall trust you."

10 Servitude

Duryodhana felt uneasy as he realised that only a few more days were left for the completion of the Pandavas' thirteenth year of exile. He had sent his spies to find out their whereabouts, but they came back to report that they could find no trace of them, producing thereby a general feeling of relief in the Kaurava camp.

The spies, desiring to add more information to please their masters, said, "During our journeys, we found that the Virata army chief, Kichaka, had been slain by certain gandharvas who were enraged at his attempt to molest one of their women." This was especially welcome to the Trigarta's chief, Susurman, one of Duryodhana's allies, who had repeatedly suffered defeat at the hands of the Virata forces. The news also produced some uneasy reflections in Duryodhana. He kept asking, "Does anyone here believe this gandharva story? Who was that woman? We should try to learn something more about those gandharvas."

Karna suggested, "Let us send out abler spies once again. Let them go round to search every mountain, village, city, and forest, and the crowds at every festival and market-place, keeping their eyes wide open. They must also pay a second visit to Virata and watch, lynx eyed, any and every group of six. They must do all this speedily, as we must discover them within a few days."

Dussasana supported this idea and added as a sort of sooth-saying, "The Pandavas must have perished, there can be no doubt about it. O brother, act on that basis and enjoy life, and do not bother about them any more."

Drona, their preceptor, warned, "It is unlikely that persons of the calibre of the Pandavas could ever perish. When they return, beware; they will come back with redoubled energy. Your next step should be to make peace with them, and also to prepare an abode to receive them. This time, send out spies who will understand the qualities of the Pandavas and look for them. . . ."

Bhishma agreed. "You should decide judiciously what must be done at the end of the short time left, taking into consideration the fact that if Yudhistira vowed to remain incognito, he would remain so, being a man of firm vows, and none of your spies will ever be able to track him. When the time comes, it may be advantageous to receive them in a friendly spirit." He added another piece of advice. "Where Yudhistira resides, the country will be flourishing. The air will throb at all times with the chanting of Vedic hymns, the clouds will gather and precipitate rain at the proper time. The fruits of the orchards will be juicy, and the corn ripening in the fields will be full and nourishing; cows will yield milk that is sweet and will become golden-hued butter at the slightest turn of a churner; people will be cheerful and contented and free from malice and pettiness. Fields and gardens will for ever be green and flowers will be in perennial bloom, the air charged with their fragrance. Let your spies look for a country displaying these qualities and when the time comes, send your emissary there with a message of good will. They have kept their word, and it would not be proper to spy on them and discover them before their time is up."

Kripa said, "Take stock of your strength and resources and increase your own powers in the short time at your disposal so that you may be in a position to negotiate a treaty with the Pandavas when they appear before you—or form alliances to fight them, if necessary. There can be no doubt that you must be in a strong position when you meet them again. After all, they are going to be deficient in troops and equipment just at this moment."

Susurman, the ruler of Trigarta, said, "Now that we know Kichaka is dead, let us invade Virata and acquire their wealth and cattle. I have often suffered at the hands of that King, and this is just the time for us to act, when they are left without a commander." He added that if the Pandavas were alive, they would be bankrupts and weaklings and not worth their notice. His own conclusion was that they had all perished and gone to the world of Yama, and no further thought need be wasted on them. Without any hesitation, he suggested that they should invade Virata and strengthen their resources and empire.

Duryodhana turned to Dussasana and said, "Work out the military details for the campaign immediately. We have no time to lose." He added, "The manner of Kichaka's death leaves no room for doubt—the hand that crushed his life out must have been Bhima's and no one else's. Only Bhima attacks and kills with bare hands. Sairandhari can be none other than Draupadi. And all that account about the protecting gandharvas must be fiction. Bhishma has described the flourishing nature of the country where Yudhistira stays. Our spies have told us how rich the Virata country is, how green its fields, how numerous their kine. All indications are there. Within the few days left, we must attack and subjugate Virata. If we expose the Pandavas before their time their exile will be extended for thirteen years. On the other hand, if we are mistaken about their presence there, we may at least enrich our coffers with the Virata wealth."

"Undoubtedly," added Susurman, the Trigartan King. "Very wisely spoken."

Duryodhana then detailed the course of action. They would form two columns, one to attack the Matsyas* first, and the other to attack their cows and seize them later. The two objectives would be achieved in the interval of twenty-four hours.

Susurman was given the special privilege of leading the attack on the capital of the Matsyas. He took the King prisoner, and carried him off in his chariot. At this, Bhima went after a tree to pluck its roots and sweep off the enemy. But Yudhistira cautioned him, "If you go on bearing a tree in your hand, everyone will know who you are and then we will have to remain exiled for another period of twelve years. Take a bow and arrow and fight unrecognized."

Bhima obeyed him. Carrying a bow, an unusual weapon, in his hand, he went after Susurman, rescued his patron and friend Virata, and also brought the other King captive. In the process of capturing Susurman, Bhima had handled him with such fury that the King presented a sorry spectacle.

Yudhistira said, "Set him free, to go back. . . ." After advising Susurman not to again engage himself in such adventures, he escorted him back to the safety of his own camp.

Meanwhile, another column rounded up thousands of Virata's cattle and drove them off. Since the Virata King, Yudhistira, and Bhima were still away on the other front where Susurman had attacked, this news was brought by the panic-stricken cowherds to Prince Uttara, who spent all his time in the women's quarters but always bragged about his military prowess.

---

* Viratas.

He thundered, "How dare they? I will recover every bit of the herd. Bring me my mail coat and arms, everyone. . . ." He hustled and pranced about in great rage. "Just watch what I do. I must rush in there and fight, only give me a proper charioteer capable of piloting the vehicle through the thick of the battle. When they see me fight, they should think that Arjuna the Pandava is in action—I have too often been mistaken for him in various campaigns. But alas, I am sadly handicapped now because I lost my brilliant charioteer in a recent campaign in which I had to be fighting twenty nights and days continuously. If I have a charioteer, I will rush like a mad elephant into the midst of those weaklings, the Kauravas, and it will be only a moment's work for me to capture the whole lot of them—Duryodhana, Drona, Kripa, or anyone else who may be participating in this cattle-snatching adventure. I am not frightened of names. I will have every one of them chained behind my chariot and bring them in a run. . . ." This was a very stimulating promise for the cowherds, but Uttara hardly made any move in the direction of the fighting field. He went on fulminating against the Kauravas, whom he called sneaks and weaklings who could be warriors only where weak opponents faced them.

All his challenging, aggressive statements were overheard by Arjuna, who was also in the women's quarters, and he persuaded Draupadi to suggest to the Prince, "Brihannala is a good charioteer. He used to drive Arjuna's chariot and helped him in many an expedition, including the famous destruction of Khandava Vana, that forest which Arjuna destroyed to please Agni, the God of Fire."

Brihannala was immediately sent for, and the Prince received him with great condescension. "I learn that you are a good driver of chariots. Come, get the chariots ready and come with me. Soon I must get the cattle back and teach those thieves in the guise of kshatriyas a lesson that they will remember all their life."

Arjuna replied modestly, "I am, after all, a singer and

dancer and a teacher of women. How can I ever steer a chariot through a battlefield?"

The Prince said, "Sairandhari and my sister both speak well of you, and I trust them. Either you are modest or trying to shirk. No time to waste. Come on. Get ready for the battle. That is my order. Don't talk back. Battle dress now, that is my order." Saying this, he donned a shining coat of mail and bristled with a variety of arms, commanding Arjuna also to dress himself appropriately for the martial occasion. Arjuna made many blunders while putting on his armour and mail coat, pretending that he did not know which was the right side of each item, all of which made the girls watching him burst into peals of laughter.

After all these pleasantries, they started for the battlefield, while the women presented them flowers and lit and circled incense in front of the chariot to wish them success in their expedition. "Don't forget to bring us souvenirs of the battle," they said.

All along the way, Uttara admonished Arjuna and advised him on how he should conduct himself in war. As the horses galloped, Uttara commended his charioteer's ability. "No wonder Arjuna could fight anywhere with a driver like you. Well, we will soon return to the capital with those Kauravas in chains and all the cattle freed. I am sure my father will have a surprise indeed, when he comes back from his campaign and finds the kind of prisoners I have brought him." Thus talking they were soon within sight of the Kaurava army, arrayed on the boundary line.

At the sight of the serried ranks as far as the eye could reach, Uttara began to waver. "Brihannala, don't drive so fast, pull up for a little while: We have to think a little at this moment. Wait, wait . . . I see Karna and Duryodhana and the whole lot of them there . . . I never expected all of them would turn up like this. . . . We must reconsider our position at once. . . ." Arjuna did not slacken his reins but, heedless of the young man's orders, drove his steeds faster, whereupon the young Prince became somewhat desperate. "Don't you hear me?"

Arjuna said, "Don't be disheartened yet. Once I set the pace I can never slacken. Let us see. Let us rush into their midst, and you will see how they scatter. . . ."

The Prince began to wail. "See the hair bristling up on my arms, don't you notice it? It means that I am not well. I cannot go out and fight in this condition. Let us go back. I need some medicine to set me right. I have forgotten to bring it along with me."

"You ordered me to take you to the Kauravas; I won't rest until I do so. . . ."

"Oh, impossible . . . driver, listen to me . . ."

"No, nothing to argue about now. Fight we must . . ."

"Oh, listen. My father has taken the entire army with him to fight the Trigartas, leaving me alone in the city. He had no thought for me. If only he had left a few men to assist me . . ."

"Do not be anxious. Why do you already look pale and shaken? You have not yet begun to fight. You ordered 'take me to the Kauravas.' I have to fulfil your command. I can do nothing less. I am prepared to fight to the death to recover the cows; or for any purpose. You showed off before the women so impressively. Now if we return without the cows they will laugh at us. I will fight, since Sairandhari expects me to attain glory. You keep still if you cannot fight."

Uttara became quite desperate. "Let them rob us of our country, if they like. I would not care. Let the women laugh at me. I don't care. Let all those accursed cows perish. I don't care. Let our city become a desert. It will not matter. Let my father think the worst of me, and call me a coward and what not. What if he calls me names?" Saying this, Uttara jumped off the chariot, flung away his arms, and began to run in the opposite direction.

Arjuna stopped the chariot, ran after the fleeing Prince, and pulled him back. "Don't run away. You drive the chariot and I will do the fighting. Don't be afraid. Now climb up that tree and fetch the bundle you will find in it."

"The tree is grown on impure ground. How can one of royal family set foot in a graveyard? And that thing dangling there looks like a corpse. No kshatriya can ever pollute himself by approaching a corpse."

"It is not a corpse," said Arjuna, "but only a sack done up to look like one so that people may not go near it. The sack contains all the weapons of the Pandava brothers. You must go up and bring it down."

The Prince had no choice but to climb the tree. When he came back with the sack, Arjuna untied the ropes and took out the weapons while Uttara watched, letting out many cries of admiration. Arjuna took out his Gandiva, his own bow, and explained, "This is the largest and greatest weapon, equal to one hundred thousand weapons, capable of adding kingdoms to its owner and devastating armies single-handed. With this Arjuna achieved his victories. It was a weapon worshipped by the gods. Shiva held it for a thousand years, and then, one by one, all the gods, and finally Arjuna got it from Agni. No mightier weapon was ever known." And then he explained the nature and origin of all the other weapons—scimitars, bows and arrows, and swords—which were used with special competence by each one of his brothers.

Uttara was overwhelmed by the spectacle before him and could not help asking, "Where are those eminent warriors? I had heard that they lost everything and became wanderers. Why, with these weapons they could have conquered the world!"

"They will," said Arjuna firmly. "And this Gandiva will soon come out of its cover."

"Where is the wielder of Gandiva?" asked the young man.

"Here," declared Arjuna, and explained who the others were.

Uttara was thrilled and cried, "My cowardice is gone. I

can now fight the celestials themselves. Let me have the honour of driving your chariot; I will steer the horses like Indra's own charioteer, Matali."

Arjuna tied up his hair and put on his shoulder plates and wristlet, and all the war paraphernalia. Uttara was aghast at the transformation that occurred in the other's personality, and felt so reassured that he said again and again, "Now I will dash through any army at your command."

In spite of this brave statement, when Arjuna blew on his conch, he began to shake with fear and collapsed on the floor of the carriage. He was unable to hold the reins because his hands trembled. Arjuna explained, "When my conch is blown, its sound always makes my enemies tremble, but you are no enemy, be calm. . . ."

"It is no ordinary sound, sir. The earth seems to shake, the trees sway as in a storm, and the birds in the air, whether it be an eagle circling high or a sparrow, collapse on their wings."

"Get up, get up," said Arjuna. "You will be all right. I will drive the horses, you just hold on firmly. I am blowing on the conch again. . . ."

The sounding of the conch shook Uttara again, but he rallied himself and soon took charge of the horses. Arjuna had hoisted his own banner on the chariot in place of the Prince's. When the banner, a divine gift from Agni, decorated with a likeness of the monkey-god, Hanuman, was hoisted, different types of supernatural beings took their seats on the chariot, uttering war cries, all of which reached the enemies' ears.

Drona was the first to say, "That conch is surely Arjuna's. He is here. We must be ready to face him now."

Duryodhana replied, "The terms were that they should spend the thirteenth year undiscovered. The thirteenth year is still running, which means they must be exiled for another twelve years. Whether it is due to their miscalculation or ours, it is up to our grandsire, Bhishma, to tell us. We did not come here to spy on them, but for a different purpose—only to carry off the cattle of the Matsya King, and to support Susurman, who may be joining our columns any minute now, bringing Virata in chains. We need not waste time in speculation; fighting is our only course. We have come prepared for it."

As usual, Karna supported his view, and revelled in visions of taking Arjuna single-handed. But Aswathama, Drona's son, sneered at Karna and Duryodhana, remarking, "I am not prepared to fight Arjuna now. No need to. After all, they have kept their pledge, and what reason have we now to fight them?" He turned to Karna and Duryodhana. "Once again, unless you employ your crafty uncle to perform a mean trick, you will have no chance against Arjuna or his brothers."

While they discussed all aspects of the question, Bhishma suggested that instead of anyone fighting or facing Arjuna, the six of them should stand together and attack him. All agreed that Duryodhana should not be exposed to this risk, and they urged him to leave the field and go back to Hastinapura.

Arjuna watched closely every movement of his cousins across the field, and the massing of their forces, and directed his charioteer to steer his way to each group. He observed the movement of Duryodhana particularly and decided to corner him.

Since Yudhistira was not there to restrain him, Arjuna was in the flush of freedom, freedom to reveal himself and act as he pleased, and to follow his inclination to rush and fight and try out all the astras he had recently acquired. Drona had been his master. He launched several arrows which brushed past Drona's ears and several others which fell at his feet. This pleased the master. "The arrows at my ears were to convey Arjuna's salutations and the arrows at my feet are his homage. This is the language of arrows. How great an archer he has turned out to be!"

Arjuna said, "I will not shoot unless Drona himself shoots first," and when he took his chariot close to him, Drona attacked him, and a well-matched, sophisticated fight ensued. Drona admired Arjuna's tactics. He matched astra for astra and Arjuna was able to attack and counter-attack with such grace that the gods gathered above to watch the fight. It was exciting, academic, and free from hatred or malice. Kripa, Bhishma, and Drona loved Arjuna but still had to participate in the battle out of a sense of duty towards Duryodhana. Their encounters with Arjuna had the appearance of a demonstration of the art of war, a friendly bout. But not so the encounter with Karna.

"You have boasted all your life of how great you are. Now prove it in action," cried Arjuna. Reminding himself of Karna's savagery towards Draupadi at the gambling hall, he mauled Karna, who withdrew in a bloody state.

Next, Arjuna noticed Duryodhana slipping away, and suddenly veered round to block the route of his escape. Duryodhana's supporters surrounded him protectively, as he had swooned. At this, one of Arjuna's mystic astras put everyone in the field in a coma, whereupon Arjuna ordered Uttara to take the glittering clothes off every person, leaving them with a minimum of covering, and carried the booty off as souvenirs for the girls in the Virata palace.

Arjuna felt happy that he could thus, to some extent, redress the indignity perpetrated on Draupadi that fateful day. "The war has ended, and the cattle have been recovered," Arjuna announced, and started back for the capital.

Arjuna returned to the banyan tree at the graveyard, and put away the weapons again. Hoisting Uttara's ensign back on the chariot, he advised him, "Let the messengers go in advance and announce our victory. Don't reveal who we are; it may disturb the King. Let the messengers announce that you have fought and won."

On receiving the news of victory, the King became jubilant. "My son has been victorious over the cream of the

Kauravas; single-handed he has fought them." He ordered public celebrations, but Yudhistira went on interrupting him with the statement, "Yes, yes, of course, if Brihannala was his charioteer, nothing but success could be expected." The King was so thrilled by his son's achievement that he did not like Yudhistira's comments.

There was public jubilation, and festivities at the palace. Crowds lined the roads to receive the hero of the day—Uttara. While awaiting his arrival anxiously and proudly, Virata thought of whiling away his time by playing dice with Yudhistira, who resisted the idea. He was in no mood for the game, but Virata compelled him with all his authority, and they played. The King continued to praise the valour of his son, while Yudhistira praised his charioteer. Finally, this annoyed the King so much that he flung a dice piece at Yudhistira's head, and blood began to flow from the cut. Yudhistira stanched it with a cloth and Draupadi immediately placed a vessel below the wound to prevent the blood from dropping to the ground.*

Meanwhile Uttara had returned and, noticing the blood, asked, "Who has done this?"

"I did," replied the King. "I wanted to teach this fellow a lesson for his obstinacy. . . ."

Uttara was aghast. Although he could not yet reveal Kanka's identity, he scolded his father. "You have done a grievous wrong, the brahmin's curse will shrivel you up."

Virata at once apologised to Yudhistira and ministered to his wound.

Yudhistira said, "O King, I understand. Those who are in authority naturally act with unreasonable severity when they are angry. However, I bear no grudge for what you have done. I have already forgotten it."

The King now turned to his son to ask for details of his

* According to a benediction enjoyed by Yudhistira, if his blood spilled on the ground, it would mean death to whoever caused it.

encounters with warriors of the stature of Drona, Karna, and Duryodhana. Uttara explained, "I did nothing; it has all been accomplished by the son of a deity. . . ." And he went on to describe how various figures collapsed on the battleground.

The King asked, "Where is that son of God?"

"He vanished immediately after the war, but may appear again tomorrow or the day after."

11 Warning Shots

ON THE THIRD DAY after the battle, Virata was shocked when he entered the assembly hall. On the seats meant for the kings were seated Yudhistira and his brothers: the courtier, cook, eunuch, and cattle and horse keepers, dressed in costly robes and wearing jewellery. Outraged at this impropriety, he ordered them all to get up and leave. Then Yudhistira announced himself and his brothers.

Virata was so overcome that he offered his wealth, cattle, and the entire kingdom to Yudhistira as a recompense for having treated them as servants. He then proposed his daughter Uttarai (Uttar*a* was the prince) to Arjuna, but he replied, "I have been moving closely with her for a whole year in the women's chambers, and I view her as a daughter. I would rather accept her as a daughter-in-law, married to my son Abhimanyu,* who will be a worthy husband for her."

---

* Abhimanyu was born to Subhadra, the sister of Krishna whom Arjuna had married earlier and had left behind at Dwaraka.

After all the tensions of thirteen years of exile, the wedding of Abhimanyu and Uttarai was a welcome change. Many kings and princes were sent invitations.* The most distinguished among the guests was Krishna, who had brought with him his sister and her son, the bridegroom. From Dwaraka, Krishna had also brought ten thousand elephants and ten thousand chariots, as well as horses and soldiers. Krishna distributed presents to the Pandavas: several measures of gems, gold, and robes, and a large number of female slaves.

Conchs, cymbals, horns and drums, and other musical instruments were played in the palace courtyard. Delicate venison and other kinds of rare meat were provided in sumptuous feasts. Several kinds of wine and the intoxicating juices of rare plants flowed profusely. Bards and minstrels waited upon the kings and chanted their praise.

At the auspicious hour, the bride was presented by the King and accepted by Arjuna on behalf of his son. As a dowry for the nuptial ceremony, Virata gave Abhimanyu seven thousand horses which had the speed of wind, two hundred picked elephants, and wealth of many kinds. The sacred fire roared with enormous quantities of clarified butter, poured in to the chanting of Vedas and mantras.

On the following day, the hall of assembly was filled with distinguished guests occupying their seats of gold and ivory, according to their importance. The jewellery on their persons scintillated and the hall looked like a firmament spangled with brilliant stars. When the assembled guests had greeted one another and engaged for a little while in general talk, a silence ensued. Everyone knew that this silence was only a prelude to discussions of the utmost importance.

All eyes were now turned to where Krishna, with his

* The names of kings who had come as guests, with their followers, runs to several hundred lines in the original text.

brother Balarama, was seated. It was a significant moment, the starting point of Krishna's leadership in the impending conflict with the Kauravas. Krishna addressed the assembly: "You all know how Yudhistira was defeated in a dice play by foul means. Deprived of his kingdom, he and his family were made to wander and suffer, all because he had given his word to remain in exile for twelve years, and then for a year more in hiding, which was perhaps the hardest part of their trials. They had to perform menial services and remain in constant dread of being discovered. Now having fulfilled their pledge to the last letter, the time has come for them to get back their kingdom, wealth, home, and royal dignity. But will they receive their due by fair means? Will Duryodhana respond to their appeal to give them back their kingdom? I doubt it. But still the Pandavas have the welfare of their cousins at heart and will not act precipitately. We must decide what we must do to regain our rights, if possible, without losing our desire for peace. Please consider the matter deeply, discuss it among yourselves and advise us. It is not possible to guess what Duryodhana may do, wants to do, or thinks of doing. I feel it will be difficult to plan anything at this stage, when we cannot fathom the mind of the other party. So I would suggest sending someone to Hastinapura, an able ambassador of courage and character, who can be persuasive as well as firm in speech, to get Duryodhana to give up half the kingdom to Yudhistira, who is not asking for more."

After his speech, Balarama, who was Krishna's elder brother, said, "Remember that Duryodhana has complete hold on the entire kingdom. Yudhistira in his generosity is asking for only half of it. But will Duryodhana give up one half? We must try to know what he has in mind and then decide on the course of action. I do not at all think that any firm speech by an ambassador is going to help; it may only provoke a conflict. Duryodhana will not easily yield what he has possessed so long. Let a messenger be chosen who can appeal with humility and win a concession; if we challenge, the Pandavas will not gain anything. Our messenger's language must appeal for an understanding. After all, Yudhistira had his kingdom but chose to gamble it away out of his own choice, in spite of advice from well-wishers who knew that he was a poor player. Yet he challenged, of all persons, the son of Suvala, known for his cleverness and deceit. There were many others in the assembly whom Yudhistira could have challenged, but he chose to play against only Sakuni, not once, but repeatedly. And so who is to be blamed for the present situation? Let us remember our own weakness and adopt a language of conciliation and not one of challenge."

A ruler named Satyaki, a kinsman of Krishna and also his charioteer, said, "I do not agree with your statements, sir. They are not true. Yudhistira did not seek to play, but was challenged. As a kshatriya he had to accept. He did not ask Sakuni to play, Duryodhana had arranged it thus. They deceived Yudhistira. However, it is all past. Yudhistira has fulfilled his pledge. Still they dispute and hold on to their ill-gotten possessions at any cost, making hair-splitting arguments in regard to the calculation of the time at which the Pandavas had revealed themselves after the period of incognito. I would ask for no charity. Let our messenger go up and say that Yudhistira in his generosity is prepared to take back only half his kingdom. They should yield to him or face the consequences. The way to appeal to them will be with arrows and not words. I will gather my forces and send the Kauravas to the world of Yama if they do not bow at the feet of Yudhistira."

Drupada, father-in-law of the Pandavas, added his voice. "Duryodhana will not give up anything by peaceful means. He is the kind to treat anyone speaking mildly as an imbecile. We cannot expect any improvement if Dhritarashtra intervenes; he will support his son in every way. Drona and Bhishma, whatever their personal views, will always support Duryodhana. The important step now must be to prepare for war. We must send our messengers without a moment's delay to all the kings—north, south, east, and west, so that we may be the first to get their promises of support." He mentioned over fifty rulers who should be approached at once. "In addition to all this," he suggested, "a man of learning and intelligence should be sent to the other camp to convey our demand clearly and firmly, without fear or offensiveness. Our envoy should not be aggressive or servile."

Krishna made preparations to return to Dwaraka with his retinue, feeling satisfied that a proper beginning had been made to reestablish the Pandavas. Before leaving he repeated, "Let us try to maintain a friendly relationship, but if Duryodhana spurns us, call me first, and then summon our allies. Then the Gandiva and all our other weapons can go into action."

The Pandavas selected a priest who was scholarly, well versed in the science of politics, to go to Hastinapura as their envoy. Simultaneously they dispatched messengers to various principalities to seek allies. Arjuna himself set out to Dwaraka to formally request Krishna's help. Duryodhana, who was aware through his spies of all the plans brewing at the Pandava camp, also sent his messengers far and wide to seek allies, and set out himself to Dwaraka to appeal to Krishna for his help. Both Arjuna and Duryodhana arrived at the same moment, while Krishna was asleep, and entered his chamber together. Duryodhana chose a good seat placed at the head of Krishna's cot and Arjuna sat down at his feet, both waiting for Krishna to wake up. When Krishna opened his eyes, the first person he saw was Arjuna and, being aware of the visitor at the head also, he spoke words that were applicable to both, general greetings and enquiries of welfare.

Arjuna stood with folded hands and bowed to him. Duryodhana spoke first. "Both Arjuna and I are your kinsmen and you must treat us with equal consideration. I was the first to arrive. The inflexible rule is that whoever comes first should receive the first attention. I am turning to you for help in the war which is threatening to break out."

"I do not know if you were the first to arrive, but Arjuna was the first to be seen by me when I opened my eyes. He is the younger one, and the code lays down that the younger person, under these conditions, should always get the first choice. I am willing to assist you both. I have in my control over a million soldiers, strong and aggressive; I could say they are stronger than I am. These soldiers shall be available to one of you, this army of a million men. To the other, I shall be available as an individual person, but I will not fight; I will just be on the side of the one who chooses me, that is all. Now tell me your choice: The junior, Arjuna, shall first speak his mind."

Arjuna immediately answered, "You must be on my side, even if you do not fight. I do not want the million soldiers."

Duryodhana was happy to get the million soldiers, feeling that Arjuna must be a fool to choose one person, who was not going to fight, instead of a million soldiers. He thanked Krishna profusely and left.

Hearing of the preparations for war, Salya, one of the most powerful kings and father of Madri, the second wife of Pandu, left his capital with his retinue and troops to meet Yudhistira and offer his support. Knowing of his movements through his spies, Duryodhana organized receptions for him all along the way. Arches were put up with floral decorations, luxurious pavilions were constructed where Salya and his retinue could rest, and where food and drinks were served liberally by Duryodhana's servants, well trained in hospitality.

Salya assumed these were all arranged by Yudhistira and

said, "Let those responsible for these excellent arrangements come before me, as I wish to reward them."

The servants rushed to convey this request to Duryodhana, who lost no time in coming before Salya to declare that he had made all the arrangements for his comfortable journey. Salya was surprised, but pleased. "Your arrangements are heavenly. What can I do for you in return?"

Duryodhana had been awaiting that question and immediately replied, "I want you to lead our army."

Salya was again surprised but said, "Very well, I shall be the leader of your army. What else?"

"I need nothing more," replied Duryodhana.

At this, Salya said, "I must first visit Yudhistira and greet him, and will join you afterwards."

Duryodhana replied, "Come back soon, and don't let Yudhistira hold you on any pretext."

Salya met Yudhistira, and they had a long talk. On hearing of Salya's promise, Yudhistira said, "You have given your word to Duryodhana and have to keep it, no doubt; but I must ask a favour of you. Will you grant it?"

"Yes," replied Salya.

"Although what I am proposing is not quite ethical, you will have to do it for my sake," said Yudhistira. "As I foresee it, there will be a single combat during the war, between Arjuna and Karna. At that time, you must drive Karna's chariot, and utilize that occasion to utter remarks and warnings that will dispirit Karna and make him feeble and irresolute. I want Arjuna to win. This is an improper request, I know, but please do it for my sake."

Salya gave his assurance that he would discourage Karna at a crucial moment and, after wishing the Pandavas victory in the coming conflict, he left.

12 War or Peace?

THE PRIEST who had been sent to Duryodhana's court was received with due honour and respect and seated properly. After all the formal preambles and the exchange of respectful greetings, the priest launched into a narrative of the situation. "Our Pandavas are not eager for a war; all that they want is their share of the kingdom, legitimately due to them. In all justice they should be invited to take their share. There need be no war; it is unnecessary. But if the Kauravas prefer a war, it will be their end, let me assure you. Seven akshaunis* have already assembled, ready to fight the Kauravas, only waiting for the command. There are others, each one with the strength of a thousand akshaunis of troops, such as Satyaki, Bhimasena, and the twins. Add to these the

* An akshauni was a fighting unit comprising chariots, elephants, horses, and infantry, running to several thousands in numbers.

mighty Arjuna and Vasudeva's son, Krishna, whose wisdom is worth all the might of eleven and more divisions. I am only mentioning that they are all there. They will return to their peaceful avocations if you so decide."

Bhishma was the first to answer. "How fortunate that they desire only peace. What you have said is all true; but your words are rather sharp. Perhaps because you are of the priestly class and employ words as a weapon, and also perhaps you have been instructed to speak thus. Everyone knows that lawfully the Pandavas must get back everything, and Arjuna is invincible once he is provoked. . . ."

At this point Karna interrupted angrily, "Oh, Brahmin, don't forget that Sakuni played on behalf of Duryodhana as agreed by Yudhistira, won the game, and Yudhistira went into exile as stipulated. If the Pandavas had won, Duryodhana would have experienced the same fate. But he would have respected the pledge, unlike Yudhistira who has now the support of Matsyas, Panchala, Yadavas,* and the rest, and on the strength of it wishes to demand the kingdom. Know you, O Brahmin, if it is a matter of justice, and properly approached, Duryodhana would yield the whole earth. If the great Pandava brothers wish to get back their kingdom, they should spend the stipulated time in the forests, and then come and ask. If they are hot-headed enough to want a war, they will learn their lesson."

Bhishma replied, "Your talk in this manner will not help. How could you forget even the recent encounter, when Arjuna fought the six of us single-handed? If we act rashly we shall suffer."

Dhritarashtra silenced everyone, and said, "No more discussion on this subject. O Brahmin, our answer will be brought by Sanjaya. You don't have to wait any further for our reply. You may depart. . . ." And he immediately ordered all the honours due to a departing messenger.

* Krishna's clan.

Sanjaya was summoned and briefed elaborately, and the concluding advice was, "Say nothing to them that may be unpalatable or provoke a war."

In due course, Sanjaya reached Upaplavya, on the outskirts of the Virata capital, where the Pandavas were residing. There he presented ceremonial greetings and good wishes from Dhritarashtra, an inevitable formality even in the worst of times. After these courtesies Yudhistira, seated in the midst of his allies and supporters, ordered Sanjaya to speak openly of his mission.

Sanjaya said, "This is what our King and his wise counsellors, Bhishma and the rest, desire—peace, long-lasting peace between the Pandavas and the Kauravas."

Yudhistira said, "Of course, peace is preferable to war. Who would wish it otherwise? But Dhritarashtra is like one who has flung a burning faggot into dry, crackling undergrowth in a forest and now, surrounded by flames, does not know how to escape. King Dhritarashtra knows what is right, but would please his son at any cost, and encourage him in his wicked course. The only sane adviser he had with him who could speak with courage was Vidura, and he always ignored his advice. Well, you know the whole history, Sanjaya. I shall seek peace as you advise. Give me back my own creation, Indraprastha. Advise Duryodhana to do this immediately and I assure you that there will be no war."

Sanjaya replied, "Life is transient, and your fame and name will live forever. I will convey your demand in strong terms, but here is my own suggestion—if they will not yield your share, I think it would be preferable for you to live on alms anywhere than acquire sovereignty by force. If you had so wanted, you once had the whole army under your control and could have easily defeated your gambling cousins and stuck to your throne. But you let that opportunity pass. Why? Because you would not commit an unrighteous act, and the same principle should be observed even now. Please avoid a war, which will result in the death of Bhishma,

Drona, Kripa, and all our elders in addition to Karna, Duryodhana, and Aswathama. Think for a moment. What happiness will you get out of this strife and victory, O Great One, tell me?"

"As a kshatriya," Yudhistira said, "I would be failing in my duty if I did not take back my kingdom by persuasion or . . . if driven to it, by force. Now I have no misgivings or doubts on this issue. However, here is Krishna, the Omniscient. Let him say what would be right, whether to fight or seek peace on any condition."

Krishna turned to Sanjaya. "Yudhistira has displayed all these years nothing but forbearance, while Dhritarashtra's sons have displayed nothing but covetousness, and now it is time to act and seek proper remedies. The entire universe and all nature functions and keeps life growing only by a proper balance of action and reaction. Otherwise, creation will collapse. You can't pretend to be better informed in codes of conduct than either I or Yudhistira. If you were so fully versed in niceties of behaviour, why did you look on when Draupadi was humiliated before the assembly hall? You never lectured on morality or law at that time. Did you make any effort then to arrest that lewd speech of Karna's? Why do you wax eloquent now on righteousness? The sons of Pandu are ready to wait upon Dhritarashtra, but they are also prepared for war. Let Dhritarashtra decide."

Yudhistira said, "We want our share of the kingdom or at least a gesture of fair play. Give us five villages, one for each of us brothers, and leave us alone. Even that will end our quarrel."

After this, Sanjaya bade a ceremonious farewell and left.

Sanjaya reached Hastinapura at night and immediately went to the palace. He told the gatekeeper of the inner apartments, "Inform the King that Sanjaya is come. It is a matter of urgency. If the King is not resting, but awake, make it known that I have arrived from the Pandavas and must see him. Do not delay." The porter came back and asked him to go in.

The King greeted him. "Oh, welcome back; why should you have waited for permission to enter, one who needs no permission, but may at all times enter?"

Sanjaya immediately began his report. "Pandu's son desires the return of his kingdom forthwith." Then he launched into a praise of Yudhistira's firmness in the grasp of virtues and concluded, "O King, you have earned a bad reputation everywhere, and will reap the rewards of it in this and the next world. Supporting your evil-minded son, you hope to keep your ill-gotten wealth and territories. When your son goes to perdition, he is going to drag you along with him. . . ."

Dhritarashtra was disturbed by Sanjaya's talk. He turned to an attendant and said, "Bring Vidura at once. I must see him this very second." When Vidura came, the King felt relieved, hoping that he would have some soothing words for him, although Vidura always spoke the blunt truth. Dhritarashtra said, "Tell me what may be done for one who has lost sleep, burning with anxiety. Advise me properly, Vidura. What course should I adopt now, in justice to the Pandavas and beneficial to the Kauravas? I am aware of my lapses in judgement, and I come to you with an anxious heart. Tell me truly what you think Yudhistira has in mind."

"Even unasked, one should speak only the truth, O Great King. Do not pursue a line of action which is clearly unjust; happiness lies only in doing the right action. He whom the gods wish to destroy will first be deprived of his good sense, and then he will stoop to perform the worst act. Endowed with qualities that make him fit to rule the three worlds, Yudhistira is waiting for your word and will be obedient to you if you are fair and just. Let him rule the world; banish your viper-like sons. Yudhistira is your rightful heir. Give him his kingdom and also yours without any delay, and you will be happy. Disown Duryodhana and you will be happy."

Dhritarashtra, somehow, did not mind this advice, but changed the topic and went on to examine some subtle philosophical points. "Sacrifice, study, charity, truth, forgiveness, mercy, and contentment constitute the eight different paths of righteousness, they say, but which one is most important?"

After answering his enquiry and occasionally throwing in an ancient tale to illustrate his point, Vidura would come back to the same refrain, asking, "If you rely on Duryodhana, Sakuni, and Dussasana to rule your kingdom, how can you hope for happiness or peace of mind?"

Dhritarashtra would dodge the issue, replying, "Man is not a disposer of his destiny. The Creator has made man a slave to fate and so what is . . . ?"

Whatever the question, Vidura would have a ready answer, and at some point sandwich it with advice to cast away Duryodhana.

Dhritarashtra got quite used to this kind of response, but slurred over it. "How are men to be classified?" he would ask, and Vidura would say, "Manu the Lawgiver has classified seventeen kinds of foolish men, such as those who strike the air with their fist or attempt to bend the rainbow. O King, the Pandavas will be your real saviours."

"The gods, men of equanimity, and the learned, prefer 'high families' . . . I ask you, Vidura, what are those 'high families' they speak of?"

Vidura would immediately start reciting, "Asceticism, self-restraint, knowledge of the Vedas, etc., etc.; those families in which these seven virtues exist are regarded as high," and would return to this theme . . . "On that fateful day of gambling, did I not tell you, but Your Majesty spurned my words. O King, cherish the sons of Pandu who have suffered untold privations in exile."

And Dhritarashtra would ask, his appetite for spiritual enquiry seeming insatiable, "What are the true marks of a

Yogi?" or "When does desire cease to operate?" For all questions Vidura found detailed answers. The major part of the night was thus spent in philosophical enquiries.

Finally Dhritarashtra admitted, "I agree with everything you say. My heart is inclined towards the Pandavas exactly as you desire, but as soon as I am near Duryodhana, it goes the other way. I am helpless, I do not know what to do. I cannot escape fate, which will finally drag me where it will. My own efforts will be futile, I know. If there is still any subject untouched by you, please continue. I am ready to listen. Your talk calms my mind."

Vidura felt quite exhausted by this time, but did not want the King to lapse into apathy and so said, "I will invoke that ancient rishi Sanat-suja, who leads a life of celibacy in the woods. He will expound to you on many other themes." He summoned by thought that ancient rishi, and after courtesies Vidura said to him, "O holy one, there are doubts in the King's mind which are beyond my competence to answer. Will you please discourse to him so that he may overcome his sorrows?"

And then Dhritarashtra asked, "O holy one, I hear that you are of the opinion that there is no death. Gods and asuras alike practise austerity in order to avoid death, which means that they believe in death. Of these which is the right view?"

Sanat-suja said, "The soul that is constantly being affected by the pursuit of objects and experiences becomes clouded." All this abstraction seemed to act as a tonic on the King. He questioned the rishi on the nature of Brahman, the Ultimate Godhood, how to attain it, and so on and so forth. The entire night was spent thus, and when morning came, Dhritarashtra was ready to take his seat at his court.

When everyone was seated, a messenger entered who announced, "There comes Sanjaya in the chariot dispatched to meet the Pandavas. Our envoy has returned swiftly, his vehicle drawn by well-trained Sindhu horses." Sanjaya was now officially back from his mission. There were formalities to be observed in his speech: "Know you, Kauravas, I am just returning from the Pandavas. The sons of Pandu want me to present their greetings before I utter any other word."

Dhritarashtra asked formally, "What message have you brought from Dhananjaya and his brothers?"

Sanjaya gave a candid account of his visit. Amidst much else, he said, "When the eldest son of Pandu chooses to draw the bowstring, his arrow will fly charged with the wrath accumulated over the years, and the sons of Dhritarashtra will then repent the war."

Bhishma agreed with Sanjaya's words, and described the divinity of both Krishna and Arjuna, who were twin souls of a divinity in a previous life. He described their background and origin, and how together they dwelt in different planes and were born and reborn together when wars became necessary, and how they were invincible. He warned Duryodhana, "You turn a deaf ear to every word of advice except that of Karna, the low-born son of a charioteer; Sakuni, the vile serpent; and your mean and sinful brother, Dussasana."

Dhritarashtra asked, "Give us an estimate of the military strength of the Pandavas and a list of those who will be their allies."

Sanjaya could not immediately answer the question; he remained in deep thought for a long time, began a sentence, paused, and fainted. Vidura cried, "O King, Sanjaya has fallen unconscious!"

"Why?" said Dhritarashtra. "What could be the reason? Is he overwhelmed by the might of the Pandava forces he has witnessed?"

When Sanjaya was revived, he described in exact terms the Pandavas' strength. There was no ambiguity.

Dhritarashtra was so upset on hearing it that he bewailed his fate. "I am tied to the wheel of time, I cannot fly away from it. Oh, cursed time! Tell me, Sanjaya, where shall I go? What shall I do? The Kauravas, the fools, seek destruction and will doubtless be destroyed; their time is up. How can I bear the wailing of women when the hundred sons of mine are killed? Oh, when will death come to me? As a fire blazing in summer wind consumes dry grass, so shall I be destroyed with all my family when Bhima lifts his mace and Arjuna wields his Gandiva. What fool will voluntarily jump into a blazing fire, like a moth? I do not feel it would be proper to fight. You Kauravas, think it over. Let us avoid this war. I have no doubt that Yudhistira will be reasonable."

Duryodhana tried to calm his father: "You should not grieve for us in this manner, as if a catastrophe had overtaken us. Do not fear, we are confident. Some days ago, I consulted Drona, Bhishma, Aswathama, and our master Kripa as to what would happen to us if war came, with Krishna on the Pandavas' side, and the whole world talking ill of us through the rumours they have spread. And do you know what the masters said? 'If there is a war, we will be with you, don't fear. When we take the field no one can defeat us,' they assured me with one voice. You must know that these giants among men will enter the sea or fire for my sake, and they laugh at your lamentations. Bhima will never be able to bear the blows of my mace. Arjuna is no match—even with Krishna on his side—to any three of us; do not overrate him because of some other experience when he defeated us at an unprepared moment. We have eleven akshaunis of troops, they have only seven. . . . Has not Brihaspati said, 'An army which is less by a third may easily be confronted'? . . . Yudhistira knows our strength; that is why he has come down from a whole kingdom to half and is now cringing for just five villages. Why will a strong man ask for less? Both the Pandavas and ourselves are of the same kind, yet why should you think that they alone will win? I promise you that the Pandavas will be seized by my friends as deer in a hunter's net, and then I will show you a spectacle grander than the one you witnessed years ago in the gambling hall."

"My son talks like a madcap or one in a delirium. Now I feel that we Kauravas are already dead. Oh, Sanjaya, tell me exactly who are the allies that are kindling the fire in Yudhistira? How is Yudhistira?" In his panic the old man could not even phrase his questions, could not even be clear as to what he wished to ask. He moaned, "Alas, that I should have a son mad enough to want to fight Yudhistira, Arjuna, and Bhima! Duryodhana, give back to them their legitimate share. Half a world is enough kingdom for you. Bhishma, Drona, Aswathama, and Salya, whose support has been promised you, do not approve of what you are doing. I know that by yourself you would not want this war. You are being egged on by those evil-minded companions of yours: Karna, Sakuni, and Dussasana."

"If you think that the elders are unwilling fighters for my cause, I will drop them," said Duryodhana. "I will challenge the Pandavas to a battle relying only on Karna and Dussasana; I will not want anyone else. Either I will slay the Pandavas and rule the earth, or they will slaughter me and rule the earth. It will have to be one or the other. I will sacrifice everything, but I will not live side by side with the Pandavas. And, my beloved father, please understand that I will not yield to them even as much territory as will be covered by the point of a needle. Let us end this useless discussion, going round and round the same subject. It is time to act."

Karna announced, "I have the Brahma Astra among my weapons, obtained from Parasurama, who imparted it to me with certain reservations. I can employ this weapon and eradicate the Pandavas single-handed."

"Your mind is clouded with conceit, Karna," said Bhishma. "You and your weapons will be squashed when Krishna decides to strike."

Karna was incensed by the remark and said, "All right, I will not fight . . . at least until you fight and die. I will not touch my arms as long as you are alive." He dramatically threw down his bow. "My grandfather, Bhishma! You will hereafter see me only at the court, not in the battlefield. When you and all the rest have been silenced and laid away, I will pick up my arms again and demonstrate what I can do. . . ." With these words, he walked out of the assembly in a rage.

Bhishma turned to Duryodhana and said, "There goes your ally, who has promised you so much support. Without his bow, how will he help you? He has forgotten how he barely escaped with his skin at Virata," he said with a laugh, and left the hall.

When they were alone, Dhritarashtra asked Sanjaya again, "Tell me truly now, Sanjaya, your honest appraisal of the strength and weakness of both sides. Does Duryodhana have as good a chance as he thinks? It must be, otherwise he wouldn't be so confident of victory. What do you think?"

Sanjaya said, "Master, forgive me; I will not say anything to you in secret. Please let your Queen, Gandhari, and the sage, Vyasa, be present when I speak to you again. They will be able to remove any ill will that my words may cause in you."

Vyasa could be summoned by a thought. When he arrived, Gandhari was called, and Sanjaya repeated over again all that he had said, assessing the strength of both sides as well as he could estimate. Gandhari vehemently denounced the idea of war, as well as her son and his allies. Vyasa, who could read the future, assured Dhritarashtra that their end was coming.

13 Action

YUDHISTIRA had a qualm of conscience. Sitting with his brothers and Krishna, he suddenly asked, "Is it worth all this conflict?" He explained his ideas again. "We should avoid a war at all costs, especially when we are certain of victory. They are our kinsmen, after all. We must make yet one more attempt to find a way which would help both the Kauravas and ourselves to live in peace. By exterminating the Kauravas, we shall regain our territories, but will that bring us lasting happiness? O Krishna, we have numerous kinsmen and elders on their side; how can we slaughter them? You will say that it is the duty of a kshatriya. Alas, I curse being born in this caste. The waves of violence never cease. Victory creates animosity; hostilities lie dormant, but continue. Even if there is one little baby left in the other camp, it will retain a small smouldering ember of hate, which could kindle later conflagration. To prevent this, it is considered necessary to exterminate the opposite camp totally. My whole being shudders at the thought. Enmity is never quenched by enmity. Confidence in one's prowess is like an incurable disease that eats away one's heart. We are ready to drench the earth in blood to establish our claims and might. It is not unlike the encounter of two hostile dogs, as the learned have observed. At first two dogs meet, tails are wagged, then comes a growling and barking, snarling and barking in answer, and then the circling around each other, the baring of fangs, and repeated growling and snarling. Then they fight and bite and then the stronger dog kills the other and tears his flesh and eats it. The same pattern is observed in human beings, too. We must make one more attempt to bring the Kauravas to their senses. Oh, Krishna, what shall I do? Advise me, guide me, please."

Krishna replied, "For your sake I will visit the Kauravas at their court. If I can obtain peace without compromising your interest, I will do so."

At this juncture, Yudhistira had another misgiving. "All the supporters of Duryodhana, vicious men, will be assembled there. I feel nervous to let you go into their midst. They may harm you. . . ."

Krishna, who was, after all, a god and confident of himself, said, "Do not worry about me. If we make this one last effort to avoid war, we shall escape all blame. If they try to injure me, I can take care of myself. Do not worry about me. I am going there only to remove any doubt others may have about the complete vileness of Duryodhana, that is all. I do not hope in any manner to convert him. I am going only for your sake. Get ready, work out the details, gather everything that you may need for a war."

"Krishna, do not threaten them," said Bhima. "Duryodhana is hostile and arrogant, but he should not be roughly addressed. Please be mild with him. All of us, O Krishna, would rather suffer in obscurity than see the Kuru dynasty destroyed."

Hearing these words from Bhima, Krishna laughed aloud and remarked, "Who is speaking? Is it Bhima, also called Vrikodhara,* or is it someone else? The hills have suddenly lost their weight and height and the fire has grown cold. How often have I seen you sitting apart, muttering vengeance, curling your fingers round your mace, and uttering the most fearsome oaths at those in Hastinapura! Is it the same man who speaks now? When the time to fight approaches, you are seized with panic. Alas, you display no manliness, but talk like a frightened child. What has come over you all? Recollect your own strength and promises, Bhima, and do not weaken. Be firm."

Bhima hung his head in shame and said, "If I have to face the whole world, I will not flinch. But now I speak out of compassion and a chance to save our race—that is all."

Arjuna said, "Peace, if it is attained without compromise, is certainly to be tried. So, Krishna, please make a last attempt." Nakula also advocated mildness in approach.

Sahadeva alone among the brothers wanted an ultimatum to be given by the envoy. "Even if the Kauravas want peace, provoke them to a war. How can I, remembering the plight of Panchali the other day at the assembly, feel satisfied with anything less than the death of Duryodhana? Even if all my brothers are disposed to practise virtue and morality, I will go up alone and kill Duryodhana. It is my life's greatest aim."

Satyaki applauded Sahadeva and added, "I will not rest until I draw Duryodhana's blood in battle and I speak for all the warriors assembled here." At this the company raised a great shout of joy.

Draupadi came forward to express her views. The backsliding of the four brothers made her indignant. "O Krishna, the scriptures declare that it is a sin to kill a harmless person, and the same scriptures declare that not to kill one who

---

* *Vrikodhara* means "the unflinching."

deserves it is a sin. Has there been any woman on earth like me? Born out of fire, daughter of the great Drupada, sister of Dhrishtadyumna, daughter-in-law of Pandu, wife of five heroes of the world, and by them mother of five sons.* Still, I was dragged by my hair and insulted by depraved men under the very nose of these heroes, and they sat silently watching my distress. I do not know what would have happened if you, Krishna, had not responded to my call for help. And now even Bhima speaks of morality. There is no one to help me . . . even if my husbands abandon me, my sons are worthy of taking up arms to avenge our wrongs. . . ." She was choked with tears and concluded, "O Krishna, if you wish to do me a favour, let your wrath not be mitigated by what my husbands say, and let it scorch the sons of Dhritarashtra." She broke down and wept.

Krishna comforted her with the promise, "Have no doubt. The wrongs you have suffered will be avenged. It will soon be their turn, unfortunately, their women's turn, to wail and weep. The day is coming. Do not fear."

When Krishna departed for Hastinapura, various omens were noticed there. Out of a clear sky came rumbling thunder and streaks of lightning; fleecy clouds poured down rain; seven large rivers reversed their direction and flowed westward; the horizons became hazy and indistinguishable. Loud roars were heard from unseen sources in the sky; a storm broke out and trees were uprooted. However, where Krishna's chariot passed, flowers showered down and a gentle cool breeze blew.

Spies had carried reports of Krishna's departure to Hastinapura, and Dhritarashtra became quite excited. He immediately ordered arches of welcome to be erected all along the route and pavilions to be put up, luxuriously furnished

* The five sons of the Pandavas were growing up in Krishna's custody at Dwaraka.

and stocked with food and refreshment, offering entertainment of every kind for the visitor and his retinue.

Dhritarashtra summoned Vidura and said to him, "I want to honour our visitor with gifts of the finest kind—sixteen decorated chariots of gold, drawn by the finest horses, each with attendants; ten elephants with tusks like ploughshares; a hundred maidservants of the complexion of gold, all virgins, and as many men-servants; eighteen thousand blankets, soft as swan feathers, which were presented to us by men from the hills who spun the wool of Himalayan sheep; a thousand deerskins brought from China; and the finest gems in our possession. All are worthy of the great, honourable visitor. All my sons and grandsons except Duryodhana will stand at the city boundary to receive Krishna. Let all our citizens with their wives and children line the route, which must be well watered so the dust is kept down." He went on elaborating his plans.

Vidura, ever a candid critic, said, "He deserves all this and more. But, O King, I know your secret purpose. The Pandavas desire to be given only five villages; you can please our visitor by yielding those five villages rather than all these luxuries and gems. You only plan to win Krishna's support with all your bribes. You will not succeed. Give him rather what he comes for . . . peace and justice. Behave like a father to the Pandavas also, as they always treat you with the utmost filial respect and affection. Krishna is trying to speak to you about the need to let the Pandavas and Kauravas live in peace. You must try to achieve it rather than offering him virgins, gems, and the other gifts."

Duryodhana understood Vidura's statement in his own way and declared, "I agree with Vidura. You must not give Kesava* anything more than a welcome of honour. And then . . . ," he chuckled to himself as he added, "We will keep him as our honoured . . . prisoner. When he is confined, the

* Another name for Krishna.

Pandavas will collapse and become our slaves. Now if you wish to advise, tell me how best to achieve my purpose without rousing Krishna's suspicion when he arrives tomorrow morning."

Dhritarashtra felt shocked at his son's words. "Never talk in that strain again. He is coming as an ambassador and has done no harm to anyone. What undreamt-of evil comes to your mind!"

Krishna was received on the outskirts of the capital by Bhishma, Drona, Kripa, and others, and citizens thronged there by the thousands. On his arrival, Krishna went straight to the palace to formally call on Dhritarashtra. Then he visited Kunthi at her residence to give her news of her sons, from whom she had been separated for over thirteen years.

She said, "When I think of it, my daughter-in-law's fate fills me with more grief than my sons'. Married to these heroic men, she yet had neither protection nor peace, and has been separated from her children all these years! How she could have borne this particular anxiety, in addition to all else, is unimaginable. Tell my sons that it is time to act. If they hesitate and delay, they will be making themselves contemptible and I will give them up for ever."

Krishna said, "You will soon see them as the lords of the earth, with their enemies routed and buried."

At the first opportunity, Duryodhana said to Krishna, "O Great One, you must eat in my house today. I have prepared a grand banquet in your honour."

Krishna replied, "No, I cannot accept your hospitality."

"Why so? With you we bear no ill will. Your reply is unbecoming."

"One should accept food only if one is desperate or loves the person who offers it. I am in no desperation. Nor have you endeared yourself to me by any act of yours. For no known reason you hate the Pandavas, who have done you no injury. He who hates the Pandavas hates me; those who love them love me; that is all. I cannot eat your food, which seems to me contaminated with evil."

Instead, Krishna went to Vidura's home and ate there. Vidura had a warning for him: "This fool, Duryodhana, already thinks his purpose is achieved with the assembling of his huge army. He is in no mood to listen to anyone. I dread your going into that wicked assembly and speaking your mind. No purpose will be served by your going into their midst again. Please keep away from them."

Krishna was untouched by these fears and appeared next day at the full assembly. There he gave vent to his feelings, and explained his mission unambiguously, offering peace with one hand and an ultimatum with the other.

Duryodhana was angered by Krishna's words. "I see nothing to be apologetic about. What have I done? I won the game. I do not see why you people find fault with me all the time, as if I had committed a heinous deed. The Pandavas were defeated in the game by Sakuni and lost their kingdom, that is all. I gave them back everything at the end of it, but they lost again and went into exile. Whose fault is it? Who compelled Yudhistira to come back and play a second time? Why do they think of me as their enemy? For what reason? Why should I be blamed for all their rotten luck and incompetence in playing? Now they seek a fight with us as if they were strong. Please dissuade them from taking this suicidal step. Tell them, O Kesava, as long as I breathe I will not give them any land, not even enough to cover a needlepoint. That is final."

"Oh, you have a blunted conscience," said Krishna. "You think that you have done no wrong. Let the eminent men assembled here judge. . . ." He recounted the history of the conflict from beginning to end, every now and then warning Duryodhana of the consequences.

Dussasana, seeing that all the elders were supporting

Krishna, said cynically to his brother, "If you do not make peace with the Pandavas, Drona, Bhishma, and your own father will bind us, hand and foot, and deliver us over to the Pandavas." At this, Duryodhana glared angrily at the assembly and walked out of the hall. Following him went his brother, his allies and counsellors, leaving the ambassador without an audience for his message.

Krishna said, "King, the time has come for you to bind and confine this son of yours with his accomplices, as Dussasana himself suggests. Deprive him of his authority and make peace with the Pandavas. Save the race from extinction."

Dhritarashtra became nervous and told Vidura to fetch Gandhari immediately. "If she has any influence on this demon, we may still be able to save ourselves."

Gandhari was brought in hurriedly, and Dhritarashtra explained the situation to her. She ordered an attendant to fetch Duryodhana at once. Then she scolded her blind husband, blaming him for the recklessness of Duryodhana, for the indulgence he had always shown him. When Duryodhana came back, she lectured him, although he breathed heavily ("like a snake") and with eyes red ("as copper from wrath"). Gandhari spoke on the futility of war and the sin of avarice, but Duryodhana spurned her advice and, even while she was talking, walked out again.

Outside the hall he consulted Sakuni, Dussasana, and Karna, and came to the conclusion that it was time for them to act. "We shall seize this Krishna by force, confine him in prison, and then fight and eliminate the Pandavas in a trice. Let Dhritarashtra cry and protest, but we shall execute our plan." Satyaki, coming to know of this plan, assembled his troops in readiness to protect Krishna, and entered the assembly hall to warn him.

When Krishna heard the news he said to Dhritarashtra, "If they wish to seize me violently, let them. I can chastise all these misguided men, but I will refrain from such acts in your august presence. I give them permission to try and seize me if they wish."

Dhritarashtra became desperate, begging for time to make one more attempt to dissuade Duryodhana from his evil plan. When Duryodhana re-entered, surrounded by his group of supporters, Dhritarashtra spoke once more to him strongly, but it had no effect. Vidura also spoke to him at length.

Finally Krishna himself said, "Suyodhana,* you are a deluded being. You plan to seize and hold me, thinking that I am alone!" He burst into laughter and said, "Now see. . . ." He produced a multidimensional vision of his stature and personality, surrounded by the Pandavas and all the gods, and all the armies of the world. It was impossible to seize any part of him. It is said that Dhritarashtra regained his sight for a moment to behold the grand vision and then begged to be left sightless again so that later he might not see the destruction of his race with his own eyes.

After granting this vision, Krishna resumed his mortal form and walked out of the assembly. When he was ready to start back for Upaplavya, all the Kauravas at the court bade him a respectful farewell. Before leaving, Krishna turned to Karna and suggested, "Why don't you come into my chariot and ride with me?" Karna immediately obeyed, with his own chariot following him.

During the ride Krishna spoke to him with extreme tenderness and tried to wean him away from the Kauravas. He explained to him his parentage; how he was to be considered the eldest of the Pandavas; how he would be the successor, as soon as the war was won; and how Yudhistira, being his junior, would be the heir apparent. Karna simply said, "I understand your love, which makes you promise me these, but, Janardana, I cannot accept your suggestion. I am indebted to Duryodhana for his support

* Another name for Duryodhana.

all these years. How can I give him up, although I know we are all doomed?"

"Your loyalty is understandable, but destructive, unnatural. You are gifted and brilliant, but you must have discrimination and understand right and wrong. Your friendship is no help to Duryodhana; you are only supporting his unholy decision, for which his death is certain." Krishna stopped his chariot so that Karna might get into his own and return to Hastinapura. Before parting, Karna said, "If I am killed in the war, I shall attain the heavenly seat kept for warriors. Once there may I hope to have the honour of meeting you again and retaining your grace?"

Krishna said, "Let it be so," and gave him a parting message. "When you get back, tell Drona and Bhishma that this month is suitable. Food, drink, and fuel are abundantly available; the roads are dry, free from slush; the weather is pleasant and moderate. After seven days we will have the new moon. We will commence the battle then."

The next day, Kunthi arrived at Karna's home to try to persuade him to give up Duryodhana. Again she explained Karna's origin, and how he was to be considered one among the Pandavas.

Karna said, "I respect and believe you, but I cannot accept your words with the authority of a mother. You found it possible to desert me and float me down the river. The parents I have known are the Suta and his wife who saved and nourished me. I will fight for Dhritarashtra's son until a wisp of breath is left in me. However, in deference to your wishes, I shall fight only with Arjuna and no one else. I will never encounter the other four at any time. I promise, whether I survive or Arjuna survives, you will have five sons left at the end."

Kunthi embraced him and wept and said, "Very well, you have pledged to spare four of my other sons. Only remember this pledge at the time you draw your bowstring. Fate, fate, what can one do? My blessings and farewell."

14 Hesitant Hero

When Krishna came back and reported the results of his mission, Yudhistira turned to his brothers and said, "You have heard the final word from the other side. We have assembled seven akshaunis of troops. We have seven distinguished warriors who could each lead a division: Drupada, Virata, Dhrishtadyumna, Sikandi, Satyaki, Chekithana, and Bhima; all of them conversant with the Vedas, brave, and accomplished in the science of warfare; all of them familiar with the use of every kind of weapon. Now I want your advice as to who should be the Commander-in-Chief. On the other side, Bhishma is certain to be the Generalissimo." Many names were suggested, but finally, on Krishna's advice, Draupadi's brother, Dhrishtadyumna, was made the Supreme Commander.

As the time for battle approached, troop movements began, creating a tremendous din—horses neighing, elephants trumpeting, their riders shouting and urging them on over the noise of drums, conchs, and rolling chariot wheels. Yudhistira personally supervised the transportation of food supplies and fodder. He gathered a stock of tents, cash chests, war machines, weapons, and medicines, and made arrangements for surgeons and physicians to follow the army. He left Draupadi behind at Upaplavya, with a strong contingent to guard her.

Yudhistira marched at the head of the advancing troops. In the rear were Virata, Dhrishtadyumna, Virata's sons, forty thousand chariots; cavalry and infantry. Yudhistira encamped on the levelled part of a field called Kurukshetra, which was at a fair distance from cemeteries, temples, and other consecrated ground. Krishna dammed a little river nearby for water storage, and stationed a strong body of troops to protect it. Thousands of tents were pitched all around, stocked with plenty of food and drink. Huge quantities of weapons and coats of mail were heaped in mounds.

At Hastinapura, the troops were mustered in millions and moved to the front. Duryodhana arranged his eleven akshaunis of troops—men, elephants, chariots, and horses—into three classes—superior, middling, and inferior. In addition to normal weapons, his military store consisted of earthen pots filled with poisonous snakes or inflammable material, strange devices for throwing hot treacle, poison darts, and huge syringes for shooting boiling oil. He placed akshaunis of troops under Kripa, Drona, Salya, Dussasana, and others. His Supreme Commander, as expected, was Bhishma. Karna reminded everyone of his vow not to fight until Bhishma should be slain in battle.

Duryodhana ordered musicians to play their instruments, sound the drums, and blow conchs. Suddenly, amid these celebrations, there were bad omens. The sky was cloudless, but blood-coloured showers fell and made the ground slushy. Whirlwinds and earthquakes occurred. Meteors fell. Jackals howled.

Dhritarashtra received a description of the armies through Sanjaya, who had been granted an extraordinary vision by which he could watch the progress of the battle from his seat in the palace hall. Sanjaya reported on the formations of troops facing each other on the east and west of Kurukshetra Field. At dawn all the arrangements were complete and both sides were ready to fight.

Piloted by Krishna, Arjuna's chariot was stationed at a strategic point in the front line from which he could survey fully the personalities opposite. He recognized each one, and suddenly lost heart. All his kinsmen, his guru, his uncle, grandfather, and cousins were there waiting to be hurt and killed. He suddenly felt weak and irresolute. He confessed to Krishna, "I cannot go on with this war. My grasp on Gandiva slips, my mind wanders; how can I slaughter my kith and kin? I do not want the kingdom; I do not want anything. Leave me alone. Let me go away." The Gandiva slipped from his hand, and he sat down on the floor of his chariot and began to sob. "How can I direct my arrow at Bhishma or Drona, whom I ought to worship? I do not know if any kingdom is worth winning after so much bloodshed. What is that gain worth?" Thus he lamented.

When Arjuna fell into a silence after exhausting his feelings, Krishna quietly said,* "You are stricken with grief at the thought of those who deserve no consideration."

Krishna then began to preach in gentle tones, a profound philosophy of detached conduct. He analysed the categories and subtle qualities of the mind that give rise to different kinds of action and responses. He defined the true nature of personality, its scope and stature in relation to society, the world, and God, and of existence and death. He expounded yoga of different types, and how one should realize the deathlessness of the soul encased in the perishable physical

* This part of the epic is known as *The Bhagavad-Gita*, an eighteen-chapter classic of Hindu philosophy.

body. Again and again Krishna emphasized the importance of performing one's duty with detachment in a spirit of dedication. Arjuna listened reverently, now and then interrupting to clear a doubt or to seek an elucidation. Krishna answered all his questions with the utmost grace, and finally granted him a grand vision of his real stature. Krishna, whom he had taken to be his companion, suddenly stood transformed—he was God himself, multidimensional and all-pervading.

Time, creatures, friends and foes alike were absorbed in the great being whose stature spanned the space between sky and earth, and extended from horizon to horizon. Birth, death, slaughter, protection, and every activity seemed to be a part of this being, nothing existed beyond it. Creation, destruction, activity and inactivity all formed a part and parcel of this grand being, whose vision filled Arjuna with terror and ecstasy. He cried out, "Now I understand!"

The God declared, "I am death, I am destruction. These men who stand before you are already slain through their own karma, you will be only an instrument of their destruction."

"O Great God," said Arjuna, "my weakness has passed. I have no more doubts in my mind." And he lifted his bow, ready to face the battle. Krishna then resumed his mortal appearance.

When Arjuna was seen to take up his bow again, great relief swept through the ranks of the Pandavas. Just when this happened and the battle was about to begin, much to everyone's surprise, Yudhistira was seen crossing over to the other side, after taking off his armor and mail coat. The Kauravas thought at first that he was approaching to sue for peace, having become nervous at the last moment. But Yudhistira went directly to his master, Drona, and bowed to him, touched the feet of his grand-uncle, Bhishma, and the other elders, and returned to his post. Wearing again his coat of mail and armour, he gave the signal for attack.

The battle was to rage for eighteen days on the field of Kurukshetra, sometimes in favour of one side and sometimes in favour of the other. It was strictly understood that action should begin at sunrise and end with the setting sun, but as the days passed this restriction was not always observed. Sometimes battle was prolonged into the night when the armies fought with the help of flares and torches. Normally they ceased to fight at sunset, and retreated to their respective tents to assess the day's action and plan the following day's strategy. The soldiers relaxed at night with song and dance.

Each day the troop formations were altered. Both sides tried to obtain information as to the intentions of the other and plan a counter-move. Several types of troop formations were ordered by the generals according to the need of the hour. If the troops on one side were formed in makara, the fish, the other adopted the form of krauncha, the heron, so that the formation and the attack thereon might follow a logistical law. The commanders chose how the troops should be placed, deployed, or formed. Each unit commander had to decide for himself how best to act under a given circumstance. On the third day, Bhishma had the Kaurava army in the eagle formation. For this the antidote was the crescent formation, with Bhima and Arjuna at each tip of the crescent, which could close from both sides in a pincer movement.

Each day there was exultation on one side and despair on the other—a see-saw of hope and despair. Counting their losses, the Pandavas sometimes felt hopeless, but Krishna, always beside Arjuna, kept up their spirits with his encouraging words. Every day on both sides there were disheartening losses of men, horses, and leaders, and the ground became soaked with blood.

15 Delirium of Destruction

ON THE FIRST DAY of battle* the initial move was made by Bhima, leading his regiment. He sprung into action with gusto, breaking out of the bonds and repressions of fourteen years. Abhimanyu, Arjuna's son, the youngest warrior in the field, joined the fray and his targets were well defined. Bhishma, his great-grandfather, was his first target, and his arrows pierced him in nine places. Bhishma, while admiring the young man's pluck, retaliated mercilessly.

Arjuna said to Krishna, "Steer me close to Bhishma. Unless we put an end to the grand old man, we will not survive —he is proving deadly." Although Bhishma had a special

* I have omitted many of the daily details of the battle, passed over routine movements, and touched upon only the more important personalities, their strategies, and the results of their actions, as vignettes of the war. Otherwise the reader is likely to feel confused and weary because of the sheer quantity of material found in the original.

bodyguard of picked warriors, Arjuna's attack was unrelenting.

Duryodhana, watching the course of battle, became nervous. He appealed to his elder, Bhishma, almost reprimanding him, "This combination of Krishna and Arjuna threatens to wipe us out. Karna, on whom I could always depend, will not fight, but only stand aside as long as you are alive."

Bhishma said, "Do you suggest that I immolate myself and leave the way clear for Karna?"

Duryodhana became apologetic and explained, "Please act quickly and get Arjuna out of the way."

At this, Bhishma shot an arrow which drew blood from Krishna's chest, but left him unaffected. The sight of it, however, enraged Arjuna and strengthened his determination to destroy Bhishma, whose bodyguards were collapsing one by one. They attacked and counter-attacked and came so close to each other that at times the chariots could be identified only by the pennants fluttering above them. But the engagement was inconclusive.

At another sector, Drona and Dhrishtadyumna were engaged in a deadly combat. Dhrishtadyumna had waited for this chance all his life.* Dhrishtadyumna's charioteer was killed by Drona's shaft. Dhrishtadyumna took his mace, jumped down from his chariot, and advanced on foot. Drona's arrow knocked off the mace from his hand, but Dhrishtadyumna drew his sword and sprang forward. Drona neutralised him again. At this moment, Bhima came to Dhrishtadyumna's rescue and carried him off in his chariot.

The Kauravas concentrated their attack on Arjuna and surrounded him, but he always kept himself within a sheath

* His birth itself, as one may remember (page 31), was for restoring his father's honour. An old score was to be settled. The dishonour, defeat, and lifelong animosity between Drupada and Drona was coming to a head at this moment.

created by a perpetual stream of arrows rotating around his person. At another part of the battlefield, Sakuni led a force against Satyaki and Abhimanyu.

Bhima and his son Ghatotkacha* fought against Duryodhana's unit, but Bhishma and Drona combined to rescue his forces and rally them. Again Duryodhana reproached Bhishma, "You were looking on with admiration when Bhima's forces were taking their toll. You are so fond of the Pandavas even at this stage! I know you can deal with them if you make up your mind."

Bhishma just smiled and said, "Do you know how old I am? I am doing my best, that's all, that's all." But he was stung by Duryodhana's graceless remarks, and went into action, attacking the enemy with renewed vigour. The Pandava army began to scatter.

Krishna urged Arjuna to action. "If you fail to attack your grandsire at once, everything will be lost. You are hesitant to encounter him. You must overcome your reluctance to touch him." As Arjuna's chariot approached Bhishma, he subjected it to a hail of arrows, but they were warded off with such skill and speed that Bhishma, although the target of Arjuna's own arrows, cried, "Bravo! Bravo!" Arjuna managed to break Bhishma's bow, but he simply picked up another.

It seemed to Krishna that they were play-acting, and he was dissatisfied with Arjuna's performance. Krishna stopped the chariot and jumped out of it, raising his discus.** "I'll kill this grand warrior myself. You will not do it, I know."

As he advanced towards Bhishma, the latter said ecstatically, "Welcome, Lord of the Universe. Let my soul be released by your divine hand; that will be my salvation."

---

*Ghatotkacha, one must remember (page 27), was Bhima's son by Hidimba, a demoness who had loved him during his sojourn in the forests. He always arrived whenever Bhima needed his help.

** The discus is used here as a weapon. Propelled by a mantra, it seeks out the enemy target and destroys by sawing off the person's head.

Arjuna followed Krishna,desperately pleading, "No, don't. Remember your vow not to use your weapon. Stop. I promise, I'll attack Bhishma. . . .

Krishna was assuaged, and by that evening Arjuna had destroyed a great part of the Kaurava forces.

At the start of the next day, in spite of their losses, the Kauravas looked extremely well ordered and optimistic. Arjuna observed their disposition and saw his son Abhimanyu plunge into the attack. He was at once surrounded by Salya, Aswathama, and a number of experienced warriors. Arjuna went up to his support, joined by Dhrishtadyumna. In turn, Duryodhana and his brothers helped Salya, and Bhima and his son Ghatotkacha came up to support the Pandavas.

Duryodhana met this array with an attack by elephant forces. Bhima got down from his chariot with his iron-clad mace in hand and attacked and destroyed the elephants. Their carcasses lay about like mountains; those that survived ran amuck in a grim stampede. While retreating, they trampled down the soldiers on their own side, thus creating a scene of immeasurable confusion. As arrows came flying, Bhima climbed into his chariot again. He said to his driver, "Ahead I see all those evil-minded brothers of Duryodhana. Drive on, we will dispatch them all; they are ready for Yama's world." He accounted for eight of Duryodhana's brothers that day, commenting with satisfaction, "The old man had forethought in bringing forth a hundred sons."

Duryodhana fought with vigour—even Bhima was hit and stunned for a moment. At this, his son Ghatotkacha hit the Kaurava army like a cyclone, and smashed them. "We cannot fight this rakshasa any more," said Bhishma. "We must stop for the day. Our troops are tired and weary."

On the sixth day, Arjuna decided to put an end to Bhishma, whose attack was causing tremendous damage. He brought in Sikandi,* placed him in front of himself, and advanced to the attack. Bhishma realised that his end had come—he could neither fight nor shoot his arrows at Sikandi, as he knew this warrior had been born a woman. Bhishma stood still while Sikandi's arrows came flying at him. From behind Sikandi, Arjuna's arrows probed for the weak points in Bhishma's armour. When he recognized the arrows coming from Arjuna, Bhishma retaliated by hurling a javelin, which was parried by Arjuna.

Bhishma decided to end the combat. Clutching his sword and shield, he attempted to dismount from his chariot, but fell headlong to the ground. The arrows shot at him were so closely pinned to his body that when he fell, a bed of arrows supported him above the ground. On noticing this, both sides stopped the fight.

Arjuna went up to Bhishma and, finding his head hanging down, stuck three arrows in the ground, lifted his head tenderly, and supported it on the stakes. Bhishma then said he was thirsty. Arjuna shot an arrow down into the earth on the right side of the fallen man and immediately a jet of water gushed out to the Bhishma's lips. It was Ganga, Bhishma's mother, who had arrived to quench his thirst.

Bhishma announced that he would lie on his bed of arrows for many days to come until his time to depart arrived. He enjoyed the boon of being able to live as long as he wished, and dying according to his own decision. After lying there a time in meditation, he summoned Duryodhana. "I hope this war will end with my departure," he said. "Make peace with your cousins without delay."

Karna arrived on hearing of Bhishma's end. He begged to be forgiven his rash words and the vow not to fight until Bhishma died. Bhishma replied graciously, "Your hatred of the Pandavas seemed too severe and unwarranted, and that was the reason for my harshness to you. You are not the son

* Sikandi (page 5) was actually Amba, a princess once rejected by Bhishma, who had assumed a male incarnation in order to fulfil her vow to kill him.

of the charioteer, but of Surya. You are Kunthi's eldest son. Go back to the Pandavas, and end this strife. . . ."

Karna, however, declined to act on this advice. "I'll pay Duryodhana with my life for all his kindness and help. I cannot change my loyalty under any circumstance." Karna paid his homage to Bhishma, and lost no time in donning his battle dress and equipment. Seeing him ascend his chariot, Duryodhana felt revived. His troops felt that victory was within their grasp, now that Karna was back in action. Before resuming battle, Drona was installed as the Commander-in-Chief after Bhishma.

Duryodhana suddenly developed the notion that if Yudhistira could be captured alive, victory would be his. "Yudhistira's capture should have priority," he ordered Drona. "I do not even want a total victory in this war; if I could have Yudhistira in my hold, it would be enough." He entertained a hope that he could involve Yudhistira in another gambling bout, exile him again for twelve years, and thus end the war.

Next day, all the Kauravas joined in the attempt to get at Yudhistira. Drona led the sortie personally. As the Pandavas knew of his plan, Yudhistira was strongly guarded at all hours of the day and night. Yudhistira repulsed a well-mounted attack by Drona with some special astras, and then Arjuna appeared and dispersed the attacking body.

Drona confessed, "As long as Arjuna is there we can never take Yudhistira. Something must be done to divert him and draw him away."

In order to attract Arjuna's attention, the Chief of Trigarta formed a suicide squad. A body of men, clad in a fabric woven of dharba grass, performed funeral obsequies for themselves and took a deadly oath before a roaring sacred fire—"We will either kill Arjuna or be killed." Marching southward, which was the direction of the world of Yama, they uttered loud challenges to their foe. Arjuna heard them and announced, "I must go now. It is my duty to accept the challenge."

Yudhistira cautioned him, "You are aware of Drona's plans to capture me. Remember this." Arjuna left a strong guard for Yudhistira and hurried away.

Krishna drove Arjuna's chariot into the midst of the Trigarta force. At first they were hemmed in by the suicide squad, but soon it scattered away before Arjuna's hail of arrows.

At the same moment, Drona approached the point where Yudhistira stood, guarded by Dhrishtadyumna. Drona avoided Dhrishtadyumna, since he knew that the young Prince had been born to destroy him. Wheeling about, he carried on his attack from another direction; but in spite of several attempts, Drona could not capture Yudhistira.

The next day, Duryodhana bitterly complained, "Yudhistira was within a few paces of you and yet you let him go. I know that you are unwilling to come to grips with the Pandavas. It is the same as it was with Bhishma. I cannot understand why you will not carry out your promises to me!"

Drona was irritated by this remark and said, "You cherish unworthy sentiments. I have already explained to you how we cannot get at Yudhistira as long as Arjuna is nearby. We will try again. Be patient and trust me."

On the thirteenth day of the battle, the suicide squad once again challenged Arjuna from the southern sector of the battlefield. Arjuna went away to deal with it, although the Pandavas could not afford such a diversion that day.

When Arjuna left, Drona regrouped his army in a lotus formation, a sort of maze in which an entering enemy would be hopelessly lost. Yudhistira felt concerned at this turn of events, and realized that Drona's onslaught was fierce and irresistible. All his supporters were desperately engaged in an attempt to crack the lotus maze, but could make little progress. Young Abhimanyu, Arjuna's son, was their only hope.

"In your father's absence," Yudhistira told him, "the responsibility falls on you. You must try to breach this formation."

Abhimanyu was willing to try, although he felt diffident. "My father has only taught me how to break into this formation and not how to come out of it."

Bhima, Satyaki, Dhrishtadyumna, and all the rest urged him on, promising to follow closely through the breach once it was effected. Abhimanyu's arrowhead pierced the formation, much to the wonder of all the veterans on both sides. He smashed his way through, overcame every obstacle, and proceeded far into the breach. But, unanticipated, Jayadratha, ruler of Sindhu and son-in-law of Dhritarashtra, moved his contingent and completely sealed the breach, preventing the advance of Bhima and the rest in the wake of Abhimanyu. He stormed his way through the enemy ranks. At one point Duryodhana himself came down to tackle the young warrior. Drona, Aswathama, Kripa, Karna and Sakuni, and a great many others combined to eliminate the young man. He met all their attacks as long as he could, but was finally killed.

On returning to his camp later in the evening, after defeating the suicide squad, Arjuna learnt of Abhimanyu's death. He broke down and cried, "I had only taught him how to break into a lotus formation, but not how to come out of it. I swear that I shall kill Jayadratha, who trapped him, before the sun sets tomorrow."

The next day, having learnt of Arjuna's vow, Jayadratha remained behind a fortress of chariots, elephants, horsemen, and soldiers until late evening. Arjuna battled his way through and reached Jayadratha, who was anxiously watching the western sky for the sun to set. The sky darkened and Jayadratha, feeling certain that he had passed Arjuna's time limit, emerged from his shelter, whereupon Arjuna felled him with a single arrow. Now the skies brightened again. It was still daylight; a false sunset had been created by Krishna, holding up his discus against the sun. He had adopted this strategy as it seemed to him the only way to bring Jayadratha out of hiding, and end that terrible day's events.

The battle had raged at many other points too. Bhima and Karna faced each other. Bhima was in his element, as Duryodhana had sent his brothers to help Karna and Bhima managed to kill twelve of them that day. Bhima felt he was born to ravage and diminish Duryodhana's prolific brotherhood, who had watched with glee Draupadi's shame at the assembly.

Karna was beaten back several times and was also disheartened at the loss of so many of Duryodhana's brothers. But he soon rallied himself and destroyed not only Bhima's bows and weapons, practically disarming him, but also his chariot, charioteer, and horses. Thus Bhima was compelled to run from shelter to shelter, even behind the carcasses of elephants, and to defend himself with whatever article he could lay hands on, such as horses' limbs, broken wheels, and pieces of wood.

Karna taunted him, "You glutton, go back to the forests and chew grass. You are not a kshatriya, but a savage unfit for a regular battle."

On this day their tempers had so much worsened that the armies found it impossible to respect the conventions of the war. Both sides discarded the time limit and fought at night with the help of thousands of torches. Bhima's son, Ghatotkacha, felt especially strengthened at night-time, as was the nature of rakshasas. He and his army harassed the Kauravas in a thousand ways. They had supernatural powers, and their strategies could not be anticipated through normal calculations. They rained arrows from unseen quarters, fought from the air above, withdrew from sight at will, and caused great damage to the Kaurava armies. The Kauravas became desperate, as they felt Ghatotkacha with his incalculable moves would destroy them completely, and they begged Karna to put an end to him.

Karna himself had been wounded by one of Ghatotkacha's missiles and was smarting with pain. He possessed a magic spear, a gift from Indra himself, which could be sent on its errand after an elusive enemy; but its potency was limited to only one use. Karna had been reserving it for Arjuna, but this day he had so far forgotten himself through pain and desperation that he hurled it on and ended the career of Ghatotkacha. Arjuna was no doubt saved from this peril, but the price paid for it was Ghatotkacha's life.

That was a crucial night all round, with fighting going on unceasingly. Drona was here, there, and everywhere, spreading death and destruction. Krishna watched his activity and declared, "We must put an end to this terrible man. He is invincible, and he can go on like this for many, many days and nights till the last member of our army is eliminated. We have to stop his fighting by every means possible. His spirit must be damped. His only sensitive spot is his attachment to his son, Aswathama. Aswathama cannot be vanquished, but if an announcement could be made that he is dead, that would be enough to make the old master pause. Who will now go and inform him that Aswathama is dead? At this moment he is quite far away in another part of the field, and we can get away with the statement."

Arjuna refused to take part in this game of deceit. One by one, each was asked and declined to utter the lie even to save themselves. They stood brooding. Time was running short. It was a matter of survival for their men and families and themselves, since Drona's attacks were unabating.

Yudhistira gave deep thought to the proposal and the situation warranting it and said, "I will go and speak to Drona.

If this piece of falsehood takes me to hell, I shall deserve it, but our cause is compelling. Krishna, I trust you. When you make a suggestion, it must be accepted. There is no other way for us at this juncture."

In order to create a situation which could give the plan a semblance of truth, Bhima picked up his mace and smashed the skull of an elephant which had been named Aswathama. Bhima then cried in his stentorian voice, "I have killed Aswathama!"

Drona heard it as he was about to discharge the deadliest of the astras in his power, the Brahmastra, which would have wiped out all the Pandavas and their armies in a second. He asked Yudhistira, believing that he was one who would never utter a lie, "Yudhistira, you must tell me, has Aswathama been killed?"

Yudhistira answered back, "Yes, it is true," and added, "but it is an elephant called Aswathama." He lowered his tone to a soft whisper while uttering the last part of the sentence, so Drona did not hear it and lost heart. He felt that there was nothing left for him to live for.

Bhima chose this moment to arraign him. "You are a brahmin, and deserting the duties of your caste, you have chosen to become a warrior like a kshatriya. You have betrayed the duties of your birth. Instead of propagating knowledge and peace, you have taught people how to use weapons for mutual destruction. You have revelled in the profession of killing. It was your misfortune that you should have degraded yourself thus."

The veteran warrior was greatly hurt by this speech, but the news of his son's death had benumbed his senses. He flung down his weapon, threw off his armour, and sat on the floor of his chariot in meditation, actually in a trance. Just at this moment, Dhrishtadyumna jumped on his chariot, and before anyone could understand what was happening, he drew his sword and cut off Drona's head, thus avenging the humiliation his father had faced years ago.

Next Karna was made the Commander-in-Chief of the Kaurava armies. Arjuna found this a propitious hour for challenging him, and resumed the battle, supported by Bhima behind his chariot.

Dussasana now approached to attack Bhima with a shower of arrows. Bhima was thrilled at this opportunity, and cried, "Now is the moment of fulfilment." He recollected the scene of Draupadi dragged before the assembly, jumped down from his chariot, and sprang upon Dussasana. Pulling him down, he tore at his hand, crying, "Is this not the hand that dragged Draupadi by her hair?" He flung the bleeding limb out to the battlefield into Duryodhana's face. Then he sucked the blood gushing out of Dussasana's body in fulfilment of his vow, shocking the onlookers, including Duryodhana.

Karna was shaken at the spectacle and stood transfixed for a moment at this exhibition of Bhima's wrath.

Salya, driving Karna's chariot, said, "I notice that you are hesitant and wavering. The situation warrants it, no doubt, but now, as a General, you must act resolutely. Don't lose heart. After Dussasana, the responsibility rests fully on you."

Karna had his chariot driven towards Arjuna and sent his choicest weapons across. A dazzling fiery arrow, called the Serpent, came spitting fire, searching out Arjuna's head. In the nick of time, Krishna pressed down the chariot and sunk it five fingers deep into the ground. The arrow missed Arjuna's head, but knocked off his crown. Red with anger, Arjuna fixed an arrow to finish off his opponent. At this moment, Karna's fated hour having approached, his chariot's left wheel stuck in the bloody mire of the ground, and he descended to lift it out of the rut. While struggling with it, he pleaded, "Wait till I set my chariot right; I depend upon your honour. Do not . . ."

Krishna cried, "Honour! How late you are in remembering this word! Where was this honour on that day when you made fun of a helpless woman dragged into your midst through no fault of her own? You did, of your own free will, choose to associate with evil-minded men, even when you could have avoided it. You revelled in evil acts, cruelty, uncharitableness, and your hatred of your brothers was blind and without cause. When all of you surrounded and butchered that child Abhimanyu, warriors thrice his age, where was this honour you talk about?" Denouncing him thus, Krishna urged Arjuna to give the final blow.

Karna now got back to his chariot, adjusted his arrow to a bow, and shot it. Arjuna was stunned by its force. As he paused, Karna got down again to lift the wheel of his chariot. When it still would not budge, he became desperate, and tried to send the ultimate astra, the Brahmastra. But at this moment, an earlier curse laid on him by his guru Parasurama—that he would forget the astra at the critical hour—became effective. He became desperate as he realised that the mantra was eluding his memory. Arjuna hesitated, since he did not really like to take advantage of this awkward moment, but Krishna urged, "Waste no more time, go on, shoot. . . . " At this, Arjuna raised his Gandiva and sent an arrow, which cut off Karna's head.

Duryodhana was advised at this point to sue for peace. "No," he said. "How can I have peace with the Pandavas, who have spilled the blood of those dearest to me, one by one, relentlessly. I will fight them to the last breath," and he did it literally, after making Salya the Commander-in-Chief.

Yudhistira personally led his forces against Salya and struck him down. Everyone was amazed at the martial capacity of Yudhistira, who was thought to be mild. Salya was one of the stoutest warriors, but in that engagement, Yudhistira displayed astonishing pertinacity and power, and did not stop till Salya's body rolled off into the dust.

Dhritarashtra's remaining sons combined to attack Bhima, but he destroyed them all with gusto, and cried, "Still the foremost enemy is alive; I will deal with him." He went off in pursuit of Duryodhana, who had lost all hope when he learnt that even Sakuni was gone, having been dispatched by Sahadeva, the youngest of the Pandava brothers.

At this point, Aswathama and Kripa came in search of Duryodhana. Aswathama was installed as the General, although only three were left alive on the Kaurava side, and seven on the other. Deeply moved by Duryodhana's plight, Aswathama took a pledge that he would wipe out the Pandava race without a trace.

Duryodhana could no longer rally his army. He picked up his mace, which was his mightiest weapon, and walked towards a lake. He churned the water apart by his mystic powers and stayed at the bottom, where Yudhistira and his brothers later tracked him down.

Yudhistira said, "Are you not ashamed to hide yourself underwater now, after all the destruction of our race that you have engineered?"

Duryodhana haughtily replied, "I was not trying to hide. I have stepped into the water to cool the fire that is still raging within me. What am I to fight or live for? All those whose friendship I cherished are gone. I have no desire to hold any kingdom. The earth is yours, take it, you have had to slaughter so many lives to get it. Take it."

"You are indeed generous, having refused me space to cover a needle-point!"

Duryodhana came out of the water, mace in hand. "I am single; I will fight you all, one by one," he said. "Surely, you have enough chivalry left not to fall on me in a pack. I am alone, without support or armour."

"Ah, how sensitive," said Yudhistira. "Did you fight one

by one with that child Abhimanyu? You did indeed act like a pack of wolves. All right, put on your coat of armour, choose any of us for a fight. If you die, you will go to heaven; if you live, you can be a king again."

Krishna felt that Yudhistira was blundering in making such an offer to Duryodhana. Since Bhima alone could prove a match for him, Krishna hurriedly urged, "Bhima, be ready."

They gave Duryodhana time to come out of the lake, and the fight began. Both Bhima and Duryodhana were experts in the use of the mace, and the fight was well matched. Sparks flew off when their weapons clashed. The fight was prolonged and looked as though it could never conclude.

While watching the duel, Krishna said to Arjuna, "Do you think Bhima will have forgotten his vow to smash Duryodhana's thigh?" Bhima overheard this at the same time that Arjuna too made a sign, and he recollected the ancient scene when Duryodhana had bared his thigh for Draupadi. He pounced on Duryodhana, brought his mace down, and smashed his thigh. As Duryodhana collapsed on the ground, Bhima stamped on his head and pressed it down with his heels, almost executing a dance over the fallen body.

Yudhistira intervened at this stage and admonished Bhima, "Enough, you have fulfilled your vow. Duryodhana was, after all, a king and our cousin."

"Let us not tarry here," Krishna said. "Soon the wicked soul of this wicked man will depart. Why linger? Come on, back to our chariots."

Duryodhana looked up helplessly, following them with eyes blazing in anger, and said, "Your base tricks, Krishna, have brought these warriors their victory. Drona, Bhishma, Karna, and Jayadratha would not have been destroyed but for your deviousness. Don't you feel repentant and ashamed?"

Krishna replied, "Your greed and hatred without reason have brought you and all your supporters to this pass. Remember, for your own good, how you won at the dice game. Don't talk of my trickery, without which you and your friends would still be burdening the earth. I have put an end to it, and see nothing wrong in stopping a war which was itself unnecessary. Now at least, let your last minutes be spent in repentance."

But Duryodhana was defiant till the end. "You profess to be a god, which I denounce completely. You allied yourself with those mendicants and weaklings and tried to prop them up. Think of me. I have lived well, never less than a king, and living as I pleased. I have enjoyed everything in life, and have nothing to regret. I have been loyal to my friends and a terror to my foes till my last second. I don't mind Bhima dancing on my body, stamping on my head—after all, my body is going to perish in a moment. What a fool to be so vindictive on a near-corpse! I do not mind all this because my future is heavenward, where warriors reach, and I know my well-wishers are there and will welcome me. You and your wretched Pandavas will be earthbound, spurned by all kshatriyas to come, when your sly, untruthful tactics are remembered. No warrior ever hit another on the thigh! Such was your advice!"

16 Victory and Sorrow

AT THE END OF THE WAR, the Pandavas returned to Hastinapura. It was difficult for them to face King Dhritarashtra and his wife, Gandhari, who had lost all their hundred sons.

Dhritarashtra asked, "Where is Bhima? I wish to greet him."

Krishna, who knew the workings of the old man's mind, presented to him an image of Bhima cast in iron. Dhritarashtra drew the image to his heart and gave it a paternal hug, putting into it all the strength of his desperation and grief. The image was crushed to pieces and fell from his embrace. Whereupon he lamented, "Oh, Bhima, alas! My embrace has proved too much for you. I hope you are not hurt."

Krishna was familiar with the hypocrisy of the old King and said, "You have only crushed an iron image of Bhima. I hope that it has satisfied your longing for revenge."

Now Dhritarashtra understood his position and said, "I am happy to know that Bhima is alive. My grief made me thoughtless. Krishna, I am grateful that you saved Bhima's life from my thoughtless act." This exercise exhausted the old man's inward rage and resentment. Now he could take a realistic view of the situation, and discuss the future for re-establishing peace in the country.

But Gandhari's grief was unabated. She turned to Krishna and lashed him with her tongue. "Are you happy now to see us all in this state? Your trickery has brought this great sorrow in our family. You have perpetrated heinous crimes on my sons."

"It was all fated thus," replied Krishna. "This was all the consequence of your sons' karma. Now that they are purged of their sins, please feel happy that they are in the heaven reserved for warriors who die heroically."

Gandhari continued to weep. "Your words hardly console me. I will know no peace until you also suffer in the same measure the consequences of your own treachery. In the thirty-sixth year from today, may all Vrishnis* destroy each other and leave you alone to die suddenly."

Krishna laughed and said, "I hope it makes you feel better to say so. I know what is ahead. Exactly in the thirty-sixth year, with or without your curse, our Vrishnis will destroy themselves in strife. I know exactly how I shall leave this world."

Now the one-month period of mourning was to be spent by the Pandavas outside the city of Hastinapura. They camped on the banks of a sacred river with Vidura, Sanjaya and Dhritarashtra, and all the women of the palace in their company, where they performed various rites for the salvation of the departed souls. When they were camping there, all the rishis including Narada and Vyasa visited them.

---

* Krishna's tribe.

Narada said to Yudhistira, "Now that you have conquered the world and perpetuated your name, do you rejoice at your victory? I hope you have overcome your grief." Narada, being what he was, knew exactly what effect this enquiry would have on Yudhistira.

"My victory!" said Yudhistira. "I have done so little to deserve it. The grace of Krishna and the physical prowess of Bhima and Arjuna brought us victory. But for me personally, it is the defeat of my whole life's purpose. All the sons born to Draupadi are slain. How shall I face Subhadra, who has lost her son, Abhimanyu? How shall I face all the mothers and fathers and kinsmen of those for whose death I was responsible?

"Apart from all this, there is one particular subject which is most painful and shocking. Till a little while ago, I was not aware that Karna was Kunthi's son. I had known him only as the son of a chariot-driver, but Kunthi has now told me his history. I have manoeuvred the death of my own brother to gain his kingdom. How shall I expiate this sin, the greatest sin among all others? I recollect I felt a tenderness for Karna whenever I looked at him. Even in his furious moments on the battlefield, even in that gambling assembly when he was so reckless in speech, I felt angry, no doubt, but I remember when I looked at his feet they resembled Kunthi's so much that I could not continue to feel angry. None of us knew him to be a brother. I had always reflected on the resemblance between him and my mother, but without understanding the reason. Why was he cursed? What is the reason for the wheels of his chariot sinking in at the last moment? You know the past and the future. Please tell me why, so that I may understand the workings of fate. Why could he not shoot the Brahmastra?"

In answer to this question, Narada narrated an early history concerning Karna. When Karna was a young acolyte, he had gone to Parasurama to learn from him the use of Brahmastra. Since Parasurama had set himself up as an implacable enemy of all kshatriyas (and attempted wholesale extermination of that community), Karna had announced that he was a brahmin in order to be admitted as Parasurama's pupil. One afternoon in the woods Parasurama was very tired and, resting his head on Karna's lap, fell soundly asleep under a tree. At this time a monstrous insect, an abnormal centipede which was actually a rakshasa in insect shape, fastened its teeth on Karna's thigh and sucked his blood. Karna bore the pain without moving a muscle for fear that it might disturb his master's slumber. Parasurama woke up to find blood gushing and drenching him and demanded an explanation, and said immediately, "None but a kshatriya could have borne this pain in silence. You have deceived me by calling yourself a brahmin, and for this grave lapse I decree that the Brahmastra I have taught shall remain in your memory until you actually find an occasion to employ it; at the crucial moment, you shall forget the mystic syllables." And Narada explained that this was the reason why Karna could not remember the Brahmastra when he tried to employ it against Arjuna.

Narada also explained why Karna's chariot wheels stuck at the last moment. "Once upon a time, Karna had inadvertently killed a cow belonging to a hermit. The hermit, enraged at this loss, decreed, 'The earth shall swallow up your chariot wheels at a critical moment,' and as a result of this curse Karna could not advance towards Arjuna on the battlefield."

These explanations mitigated to some extent Yudhistira's grief, but still his heart was heavy with repentance. He turned to Arjuna and said, "Our so-called enemies have acquired merit and are in heaven now, while we are made to live long in this hell of repentance for all the slaughter. Grief alone is our reward! Don't tell me again it is the duty of a kshatriya to kill. I do not want to be called a kshatriya if slaughter alone is the rule of life. Let me be a mendicant, far happier if I could think that I had exercised compassion and forgiveness than attained all this victory. Like dogs fighting for a piece of meat, we have fought and destroyed our blood relations. We were driven to it through Duryodhana's reasonless, undiminishing hatred, but now we have no joy outliving him in this manner. Oh, Arjuna, you become the King of this country. Let me go to the forests to lead a life of renunciation. I will live with no possessions, no aim, with only trees and innocent creatures of the forest for company." He revelled in a vision of ascetic life—to live on fruits and roots, enough to keep one's body alive; renouncing speech; renouncing all judgement of good and bad, never telling anyone what to do, never resisting anything; walking in one direction, without looking back or forward with head bowed in humility, never noticing in which direction or country he was moving.

Yudhistira went on elaborating the picture of his life as a recluse in such detail that Arjuna could not help interrupting him in anger. "Oh, that will do," he said. "Having sacrificed so much, so many lives, and acquired a kingdom, it is your duty to rule it, lest it should fall into lesser hands than yours and suffer. It is your duty to rule and enjoy, support the poor, support sacrifices, and maintain God's justice as a ruler. You will never be able to achieve this unless you have kingly power, acquired by the legitimate means decreed for a kshatriya. You will never be able to discharge your duties in this respect unless you have prosperity and wealth. A pauper can never help others, a weakling can be of no use to his fellow men. A life of renunciation is only for mendicants and not for us. A man possessed of wealth is regarded as learned and worthy of respect; wealth brings about more wealth. Religious activities, pleasure, enjoyment, and every fulfilment of life proceed from wealth. He who has no wealth is spurned in this world as well as in the next. Quarrels and differences of opinion have their place even in heaven among the gods. When this is so, what is wrong if, in our human society too, there are also differences and fights. It is by fighting that glory is earned and from glory proceed all the good things of life. It is all known as the gift of the goddess Lakshmi, and he who spurns such a gift offends the Goddess. Remember, we can never see wealth acquired without some harm or injury to others."

Yudhistira still repeated his philosophy of renunciation. His ascetic outlook infuriated Bhima, who said, "Great brother and elder, please stop your narration. Your mind is unbalanced and you have lost sight of realities. You are like the parrot-like repeaters of the Vedas, who go on babbling without relevance. If you think so ill of the duties of a king, all the slaughter of Dhritarashtra's family which you led us to perpetrate was uncalled for. If we had known that this was your philosophy, we would never have consented to take up arms against anyone. Having slain our enemies, it is your bound duty to take up the reins of this kingdom and rule like a true kshatriya. However much you may dislike it, you cannot alter your caste now. Your action is similar to that of a man who has dug a well, and, after smearing himself with wet mud, retreats from the activity just when water is springing up. You are like a man who, having killed all his fearful enemies, finally also commits suicide. We have followed you and now realise that your intelligence is questionable. Please consider our position also. You are selfish in pampering your own feelings. A life of renunciation should be adopted only by kings who are incurably diseased or suffering from defeat. If renunciation and passivity are the greatest of virtues, then mountains and trees should be the most virtuous in creation, for mountains and trees always lead a life of aloofness and do not cross anyone's path."

The twins, the most junior, added their voices, also with great trepidation. And Draupadi, who had been listening all along, added, "These brothers of yours have been lecturing and crying till their throats have dried up. You make them unhappy by your obstinacy. These brothers of yours have continuously suffered for so many years, all because of their devotion to you. Why, when you were at Dwaitavana suffering all the cold and the heat and the wind, did you not say to me, 'We shall fight for our rights, slaughter Duryodhana, and enjoy this earth as rulers once more.' You promised that our hardships would be forgotten when we reattained our kingdom. You yourself swore so much; why do you back out of it now? My mother-in-law one day addressed me and said, 'Yudhistira will always keep you happy and well provided.' Now, after slaying thousands of men, I see that you are attempting to make that promise futile. When the eldest brother is mad, all those who follow him are also compelled to become mad. If your brothers had their own judgement left, they should have immobilised you, kept you in captivity, and taken upon themselves the sovereignty of the earth. The man who is afflicted with madness must be treated by a physician and not obeyed. I am the most miserable among all, but still I have the desire to live, even though I have lost all my children. You should not ignore my words or those of your brothers."

Arjuna now expounded the duties of a king as a chastiser. "What a king holds in his hand is called danda, because it restrains and punishes the wicked; it is only the fear of punishment that will keep most persons on the path of truth, obedience, and discipline. Without piercing, no fisherman can ever succeed in catching a fish. Without slaughter nothing can be achieved. Those among the gods who are fierce are most respected—Rudra, Skanda, Agni, and Varuna are all slaughterers. All people quail before them. I see no creature in this world that supports life without injuring another. Animals live upon animals, the stronger upon the weaker. The cat devours the mouse, the dog devours the cat, the dog is eaten by the leopard, and all things again are devoured by Death. Even ascetics can never support their lives without killing creatures. In water, on earth and vegetables there are many lives which are minute and invisible, but they are killed when the ascetic takes his nourishment. This kingdom is ours now. Our duty is to cultivate happiness and rule the earth, employing the danda when necessary."

Yudhistira allowed everyone to express his views, but rejected the outlook and philosophy of his brothers and wife, doggedly repeating his plan to go into the woods and do penance. At this moment Vyasa intervened. "You must practise the duty enjoined upon you as a king. There is no other way. Retirement is not for your order. You must adopt a kingly life, a domestic life, and a kshatriya life. Stop thinking negatively. You have to rule the kingdom that has come to your hands. There is no choice for you. Be cheerful and accept it."

Yudhistira went on lamenting the death of each one of his adversaries, one by one, and kept asking, "How am I to atone for this, how am I to atone for this?" He thought particularly of Bhishma, on whose lap he had played as a child. "When I saw him attacked by Sikandi, and found him trembling and shaking throughout the attack, when I saw his body pierced by arrows and falling down like a stricken tower on the floor of his chariot, my head reeled and my heart was wrung in pain. He had brought us up and I had to arrange for his destruction through my covetousness. Drona, my master, who took my hand and taught it to hold a bow . . . how can I forget these scenes and parade myself as a king?" He tormented himself with such memories again and again. More than all other memories, the echo of the lamentations of the women on receiving news of the casualties was too much for Yudhistira.

Krishna finally lost patience with him. "It is unseemly to pamper your grief. You cannot go on like this for ever. Forget yourself and your own feelings and act for the sake of those who have gone through so much suffering in obedience to your orders. You will have to accept the kingdom."

Yudhistira suddenly realised the reasonableness of their arguments and said, "O Krishna, my mind is clear now. I obey your command, as well as our grandsire, Vyasa's. Let us now proceed as you desire."

After offering prayers to the gods, Yudhistira ascended a chariot yoked with sixteen bullocks bearing special auspicious marks, covered with satin and silk, and sanctified with mantras. Bhima held the reins of the animals, Arjuna held an umbrella over the King's head, Nakula and Sahadeva stood on the sides and fanned the King with yak tails. Kunthi and Draupadi followed in a chariot driven by Vidura. Krishna and Satyaki and many others were in the procession. The streets were festooned with greenery and flowers and perfumed water was sprinkled all along the path, and the gates of the city were adorned as never before when Yudhistira entered. The city was alive with music and the roar of cheering from the crowds.

Passing through the multitudes jostling in the main streets, Yudhistira finally entered the palace of Dhritarashtra. Yudhistira, as the King, went up to the household gods and worshipped them. He then took his seat on a golden throne, facing east. On another golden seat, facing him, sat Krishna and Satyaki. On either side of the throne were Bhima and Arjuna. On an ivory seat Kunthi sat, with Nakula and Sahadeva by her side. Dhritarashtra was given a special seat. Yuyutsu, the only son of Dhritarashtra left alive, who had crossed over to the Pandava camp at an early stage of the battle, was seated beside him with Sanjaya and Gandhari. Important citizens approached the King with presents. Jars of holy water and vessels of gold and silver inlaid with gems were arrayed around the altar.

Yudhistira, with Draupadi at his side, lit the holy fire and poured libations into it, repeating the mantras chanted by the priests. Krishna poured holy water out of his conch and anointed Yudhistira. Drums were beaten and Yudhistira was cheered again and again.

Acknowledging it all, Yudhistira warmly proclaimed, "King Dhritarashtra is still the head of our country. If you wish to please me, show him your respect and obedience as unwaveringly as ever. You must bear in mind this request of mine. The whole world, including ourselves, belongs to him, remember."

Yudhistira announced that Bhima was the yuvaraja, his next in command. He appointed Vidura his counsellor in all matters pertaining to war, peace, defence, and administration. Sanjaya was to look after the finances of the state. Nakula was in charge of the register of the armed forces. Arjuna was to defend the country and "chastise the wicked," a task appropriate to his philosophy. Dhaumya was to be the Chief Royal Priest, managing all the religious affairs of the palace and the state. Yudhistira chose Sahadeva to be his personal companion and aide at all times, feeling that the youngest needed his own protection. He appointed Yuyutsu, the only son left to Dhritarashtra, to be in special charge of the old King and to see that his wishes were fulfilled at all times.

Epilogue

WITH THE CORONATION of Yudhistira and all the tranquillity following it, one would have thought there was nothing more to say; but it is not so. The writer of the epic has a disinclination to conclude a story. Just as all the action seems to be ending, one suddenly realises that the last line is only the beginning of a new phase of the narrative, of fresh thoughts and experiences. There is a reluctance to close the subject. This may be one way of creating a semblance of life itself, which is apparently endless. Nothing is ever really conclusive.

Yudhistira, after his enthronement, found Krishna rather reflective and moody and enquired as to the cause of this state. Krishna said, "I realise that with the coming of Uttarayana,* Bhishma will give up his life. He is a storehouse

* Uttarayana is the time in the middle of January when the sun changes its direction from south to north.

of knowledge of the world, kingship, and human conduct; and when he passes away, it will be gone with him, and the world will be the poorer. I want you to meet with him. There is not much time left." Yudhistira was doubtful how he would be received by Bhishma, but Krishna went in advance and prepared the old master for this meeting.

Lying on his bed of arrow heads, Bhishma received Yudhistira with much affection and spoke to him on the duties of a king.* The discourse continued for several days. At the end of it, Bhishma bade everyone farewell and breathed his last. Yudhistira took his body off the arrows and performed the obsequies due the eldest member of the family. He cremated the body on the banks of the Ganges, where the deity of the river, Ganga, Bhishma's mother, once again appeared to receive his soul and conduct it to his original home in the realm of the celestials.

Yudhistira ruled for thirty-six years, at the end of which his old uncle, Dhritarashtra, expressed a desire to adopt vanaprastha and retire into the woods with Gandhari and his brother's wife, Kunthi, to spend the rest of his life in contemplation. Yudhistira made every arrangement for such a retirement and visited them often at their retreat and looked after their welfare—until one day, a forest fire started, and in that conflagration, Dhritarashtra, Gandhari, and Kunthi perished.

Krishna's clan, the Vrishnis, destroyed each other in a civil war, and became less than a memory, leaving no trace of themselves. Krishna himself departed as he had prophesied. On the bank of a river, while he was resting in deep thought, lying on the sands, a hunter from a distance mis-

* This part of *The Mahabharata* is known as *The Shanti Parva* (the section that calms), and contains the essentials of human conduct and outlook, as expounded by the dying Bhishma.

took the soles of his feet for a bird and shot an arrow, thus ending the tenure of the eighth avatar of Vishnu on earth.

Depressed by the news of the death of Krishna and the Vrishnis and the submerging of Dwaraka in the sea, the Pandavas decided to leave the world. One by one, the Pandava brothers and Draupadi died. Vidura had such a devotion to Yudhistira that at one point by his yogic power he transmigrated into Yudhistira's soul and merged with it.

Yudhistira alone was gifted with the power to reach heaven in his physical body. The story describes Yudhistira's passage to heaven, the peep he has into the glooms of hell, and his discovery of many familiar faces there.

At the end of *The Mahabharata* story, the stage becomes blank and not a single familiar character is left except Abhimanyu's child, who had had the protection of Krishna even when he was in his mother's womb. He grew up to be crowned the King of Hastinapura and thus continue the Pandava lineage.

GLOSSARY

ashram—hermitage

astra—weapon, missile, or arrow powered by supernatural forces

aswametha—grand sacrificial ceremony performed by victorious kings

asura—a demon

bhiksha—alms

brahmin—a member of the priestly caste

Brihaspathi—the High Priest and preceptor of gods, known for his intelligence and wisdom

danda—staff of authority (mace)

desa—country

dharba—a stiff grass generally collected for ritual purposes

dharma—established order, rule, duty, virtue, moral merit, right justice, law (in an eternal sense)

gandharva—a supernatural being

Gandiva—Arjuna's bow

guru—teacher

karma—Fate; also consequences that follow from one's actions in this as well as previous lives

Kaurava—the clan to which the chief characters belong

kshatriya—a member of the warrior caste

Kuru—another name for the clan to which the chief characters belong

mantra—syllables with magic potency

parva—part

Puranas—source books of mythology, said to be older than the Vedas

rajasuya—grand sacrificial ceremony performed by victorious kings

rakshasa—a demon
rishi—a saintly man
sama vedas—scriptures
shastra—scriptures
suta—a chariot driver
swayamwara—the occasion when a girl makes her choice among suitors
tapas—concentrated meditation over a prolonged time for spiritual growth, spiritual powers; penance
Upanishads—Sanskrit spiritual treatises
vana—forest
vanaprastha—a forest hermit
Vedas—scriptures
yaksha—a demi-god
yuga—any of the four ages in the duration of the world, each of which lasts for 3,000 celestial years (one celestial year equals 3,600 years of human time) and possesses special characteristics of good and evil